THE
LAST COINCIDENCE

• A NERO WOLFE MYSTERY •

THE
LAST COINCIDENCE

Robert Goldsborough

BANTAM BOOKS
NEW YORK • TORONTO • LONDON • SYDNEY • AUCKLAND

The author wishes to thank the estate of the
late Rex Stout for their cooperation and support.

THE LAST COINCIDENCE
A Bantam Book / December 1989

Library of Congress Cataloging-in-Publication Data
Goldsborough, Robert.
The last coincidence / Robert Goldsborough.
p.   cm.
"A Nero Wolfe mystery."
ISBN 0-553-05383-3
I. Title.
PS3557.03849L37   1989
813'.54—dc20   89-15133
                                                CIP

Published simultaneously in the United States and Canada

PRINTED IN THE UNITED STATES OF AMERICA

BG   0 9 8 7 6 5 4 3 2 1

To John McAleer,
for his consistent support
and encouragement

ONE

Okay, so the *Times* called it the best Broadway musical of the year; this wasn't the first instance where that esteemed journal and I found ourselves on opposite sides of the fence. I had gone only because Lily Rowan was aching to see the show, and as it turned out, she didn't enjoy it all that much either.

The way Lily was acting that night, though, she probably wouldn't have enjoyed Caruso at his peak. She'd been uncharacteristically quiet all through a superb dinner at Rusterman's—we each had the trout Montbarry that Nero Wolfe introduced to the menu years ago when he was overseer of the restaurant following his old friend Marko Vukcic's death. And even during what I thought were the show's few good moments, the best she could generate was halfhearted applause or a weak chuckle. She never even gave my ribs a gentle jab with her elbow, which is one of her trademarks when she's having fun at the theater.

"At the risk of stating the obvious, you're a long way from the vivacious and scintillating companion I have grown to respect, revere, and, yea, even adore," I told her in the taxi headed for her apartment on East Sixty-third just off Park. The response I got was a faint smile.

"Oh . . . I know, Archie, I'm out of sorts. I was hoping the show would jolt me out of it—no such luck. Sorry."

"Whoa, you don't have to apologize to me, of all people. Think of the many times when I've been preoccupied because of some case the Great Man and I were buffaloed by. Do you want to talk about it?"

She screwed up her face and shrugged. "No, I . . . Oh, why not, for Lord's sake? Come on up for a nightcap."

I paid the driver and we breezed into the lobby of Lily's building, which looks like it was furnished by somebody with a brother who owned a white-marble quarry. The hallman, who's been working there for all of a hundred years, gave his usual salute and his usual " 'Evenin', Miz Rowan . . . 'evenin', Mr. Goodwin," making a big flourish out of running over and punching the elevator button for us. A clear-cut example of Lily's lavish Christmas tip paying off.

As many times as I've been in Lily's palace, I still find myself gawking like a rube at the artwork and the rest of the decor. Lily Rowan and I are what the gossip columnists would probably term "old friends," which is true as far as it goes. The fact is, we *are* old friends, although that's never stopped either of us from enjoying the company of other members of the opposite sex. If you're looking for any more details about our relationship, you've come to the wrong place. And if you think she'll give you any more details than I will, forget it.

Anyway, to get back to Lily: Her late father ventured over from Ireland long before I'd left Ohio in search of fame and fortune in Manhattan, and he quickly got himself involved in both Tammany Hall— that's the old Democratic organization—and the construction business. As I've pieced it together from Lily and from Lon Cohen of the *Gazette,* Rowan made a mint building sewers in New York. A sizable chunk of that fortune dropped on Lily, who has shown she knows how to use it. A few examples are her weekend hideaway up in Katonah, her ranch in Montana, and some pricey pieces of French Impressionist art in her

New York apartment. To give you an idea what I mean, before I knew Lily, names like Monet, Renoir, and Cézanne meant about as much to me as Rosencrantz and Guildenstern.

One more thing: Despite Lily Rowan's money, however much that is, when she's out with me, I pay. Just so that's on the record.

I got myself settled on one of the three white couches in her living room with the Scotch and water I'd mixed at the bar in the corner of the room, while Lily sat opposite me, tucked her luscious legs under her, and took a deep breath, contemplating her own Scotch. Then she looked up with those dark blue eyes.

"Escamillo," she said, using a nickname that dated to when she watched me make the acquaintance of a bull in a pasture, "I need to talk to somebody—you, really—but it means breaking a confidence."

"That's got to be your call, but I think you know that I'm walking around with a lot of secrets that never got any further than here." I tapped the side of my head.

"I know, and I can't tell you why I'm hesitating except that this involves Noreen."

"Your niece?"

Lily nodded, chewing on her lower lip. Noreen James is the daughter of Lily's half-sister, Megan James. I'd only met her a few times, but that was enough for me to form a very positive impression of the young woman, who was now a couple of years out of college.

"Drugs?" I asked.

"No—at least not that I'm aware of. Please let me . . . go slowly with this," she said, stopping to take a healthy swallow of her drink. She contemplated the Renoir on the opposite wall before going on. "I think you know Noreen and I are pretty close. For one thing, she's nicer by miles than her mother, but then, you're well aware of how I feel about *her*."

I am indeed. Lily and her somewhat-older half-sister have never made a pretense of relishing each other's company, and it's easy to see why. While Lily is outgoing, free-spirited, flip, irreverent, and—by her own admission—lazy, Megan is brittle, tense, bustling, and generally disapproving of others. I have been around the lady just enough to know that she's about as much fun as being stuck in traffic with a New York cabbie who has opinions about everything and is determined to share them.

"Anyway, Archie, Noreen and I get together every so often, just to talk. She's always confided in me more than in her mother, which hasn't improved what's left of my relationship with Megan—not that I much care, of course. We usually meet about once a month."

"So you've mentioned before—at the Plaza, right?"

Lily allowed herself the slightest shadow of a smile. "Noreen loves the Palm Court. But the last two times we've had lunch, she's been a different person than anything I've ever seen before. You know how bubbly and alive and rosy-cheeked she is, or rather, was. When I saw her a month ago—it was the last Saturday in June—I couldn't believe it. She looked . . . haggard— that's the only word I can think of. Like she hadn't been sleeping. And she was distracted. She usually loves to hear the latest dirt about what you insist on referring to as the 'chichi crowd'—actually, I think she looks to her good old Aunt Lily as comic relief. We usually laugh our way through the Chablis and salad. But not that time. She didn't seem to want to talk at all, and when I asked her if anything was bothering her, she just said the job was unusually hectic."

"At the publishing house, isn't it?"

"Melbourne Books, yes. She's always loved being an editor. But when I questioned her on what was wrong there, all she would say was that she didn't want to go into it, so I backed off. She gets more than enough prying from her mother.

"But when I saw her again last Saturday, it was a repeat of the month before. She looked just as bad as she had before—maybe even a little worse. She wasn't the least bit interested in my stories, and believe me, at least a couple of them were dandies. For that matter, she wasn't inclined to do any talking herself. This time, though, I decided to press her. At first, she stuck to her earlier story about job pressures, but I wasn't buying any more of that. I have to confess that I really bore in on her—like her mother might have done if she hadn't been vacationing on the Riviera for the last six weeks. In fact, Megan is due home today, although I haven't heard from her. Anyway, then it came out like a flood, and with lots of tears."

Lily leaned back and closed her eyes. I refilled both our drinks, then sat down, ready to give her all the time she wanted.

"At this rate, I'll keep you here till dawn waiting for me to finish," she said ruefully, blinking. "Well, you've probably figured it out by this time, but Noreen was . . . she got . . . attacked." She shook her head and ran a hand through her dusty-blond hair. "And the worst part, it was somebody she knew—she was out with him when it happened, for God's sake!"

"Date rape," I said quietly.

She cringed. "What a hideous term."

"For a hideous act. Who the hell did it?"

"She wouldn't tell me. I had enough trouble getting as much out of her as I did, but I can make a pretty good guess. She's been seeing at least a couple of guys. One's a nice boy—at least I *think* he's nice . . . now I'm not so sure about anybody—she met through her brother Michael and who works down on Wall Street. The other is . . . I hate to say it—Sparky Linville."

"The wild one who's in the news a lot?"

For an answer I got a quick nod and a grimace. "In the last few months, Noreen's occasionally been with a 'too-rich-too-soon' crowd—Linville among them, although I don't think they went out very many times. You asked about drugs; I can't say for sure, of course, but I don't believe Noreen's into coke, or whatever else the high-livers are destroying themselves with these days. I wouldn't bet on some of the others, though, including Linville. I've met him only two times, and, Archie, we're talking world-class jerk here. His arrogance gives the term 'self-assured' a bad name. But I think Noreen liked the excitement of being with him, of going to the hot clubs, that sort of thing. It had to be fun being with someone who's recognized by every doorman and maître d' in town."

"And I gather you think he's the one who—"

"I'm sure of it. After Noreen spilled out what happened, I tried to get a name. She clammed up—she was almost hysterical until I promised not to tell a soul. By this time, damn near everybody in the place was staring at us. She said nobody else knows anything about it, not even Megan. But the way she reacted when I mentioned Linville's name—I know it was him."

"Obviously Noreen isn't about to bring any charges."

Lily shook her head again. "From what little I was able to worm out of her, she seems to think that what happened was somehow her fault."

"What do you think?"

"I think her reaction is what you would naturally expect in a male-dominated society where women who get attacked end up being accused of leading men on by their dress or their gestures or simply by breathing. Try to deny that." She glared at me.

"I can't. You're absolutely right."

"Oh, didn't mean to come down on you, of all people," she said softly. "But I'm livid about this, and I feel so helpless. Noreen is a great girl, so bright and enthusiastic and full of life, and it's as if she's been destroyed."

"In a sense, part of her probably has. Certainly her level of trust will never be the same, and that's only for starters."

"Which is just as well," Lily said bitterly. "Men can't be trusted, present company more or less excluded."

"Thank you for that, anyway." I gave her a lop-sided grin. "Now that you've gone on record, I'll say something that may cause you to reassess me and my sensitivity: Are you absolutely convinced that your niece is an innocent victim?"

I got a long, fierce look from under lowered eyebrows. "Okay," Lily said, setting her chin, "I suppose you had to ask. After all, you *are* a detective: the need for facts and all."

"And impressions."

"Do you think for an instant if I felt Noreen had been leading that ass on, I would have brought this up to you in the first place?"

"Point taken. But as you so articulately remarked, I had to ask," I said, getting to my feet. "I must be going. If it makes you feel any better, it probably did Noreen a world of good to finally share this night-mare with somebody—particularly you."

She sighed. "Well, I know it did *me* a world of good to share it tonight, even if I did violate a trust in the process. But that doesn't bother me in the least, given my confidante. Speaking of which, my confidante —and I ask this, still having complete faith in your sensitivity: Do you have any advice?"

I stood in the foyer and shrugged. "For you? I'm afraid not, at least at the moment. I do have some for somebody else, though, and I'm going to deliver it in person."

"Not to Noreen?" Lily said, a shocked expression on her face.

"No, not to Noreen—I wouldn't do that, and you know it. But tomorrow I plan to pay a visit to a Mr. Sparky Linville."

TWO

The next day began quietly enough. At seven-forty-five I was at my small table in the kitchen of Nero Wolfe's brownstone on West Thirty-fifth Street near the Hudson, which is the place I've called home for more than half my life. And that small table is just about the only spot I ever have breakfast unless I'm with Lily at her Katonah retreat or find myself in jail, which, truth to tell, has happened more than once in the years I've been collecting paychecks signed by Nero Wolfe. I had finished a tall glass of freshly squeezed orange juice and one cup of black coffee and was starting in on a second cup, to go with the Canadian bacon and pancakes with wild-thyme honey that Fritz Brenner was preparing for me.

Wolfe, true to his morning custom, took nourishment on a tray up in his room, and my meal company, as usual, was the *Times,* which was propped up on the rack I had had made so I could read and still have both hands free to tackle the meal. Fritz, chef extraordinaire and the one indispensable cog in the machinery of the brownstone—with the possible exception of Wolfe himself—quietly scurried about making preparations for lunch: baby lobsters with avocados.

Fritz and I have worked out a series of accommodations over the years that allow us to coexist beautifully in the brownstone. One is that he doesn't talk to me during breakfast, and I don't tell him how to cook; simple, but it works. The *Times* wasn't holding my interest, especially with the Mets wallowing in fifth place and the Yankees doing no better and also behaving as if they actually were fond of their current wimp of a manager.

After the events of the previous night, though, nothing less than an article on the latest adventures of Sparky Linville would have satisfied me. Lily had done her best to talk me out of seeing him, but I tried to assure her I wasn't going to involve her niece in any way. She had frowned and remained doubtful about the undertaking, and before we parted made me promise that Noreen's name would under no circumstances be mentioned.

I finished breakfast and carried a cup of coffee down the hall to the office. Wolfe wasn't there, of course, and wouldn't be until eleven. His unvarying Monday-through-Saturday schedule calls for him to spend four hours daily—nine to eleven in the morning and four to six in the P.M.—playing with his ten thousand orchids in the greenhouse on the fourth floor, along with Theodore Horstmann, the crotchety old orchid tender who's worked for Wolfe even longer than I have.

I touched down at my desk and contemplated the day's work, which consisted primarily of paying the bills and updating the orchid-germination records on the personal computer. We didn't have any cases at present, which suited Wolfe just fine, what with his case of terminal laziness. The bank balance was reasonably healthy, though, in the main because of the fat fee our fat resident genius got for figuring out— with some incidental help from yours truly—which of a Scarsdale millionaire's domestic staff of seven had filched a coin collection valued in the high six figures.

After contemplating the day's chores some more, I put them aside and dialed Saul Panzer's number. For those of you new to these narratives, Saul is a free-lance operative, or detective if you prefer, the best of his kind in New York City and, for my money, in the western hemisphere, maybe the eastern too. Anyway, Nero Wolfe has hired him for everything from a basic tailing job to putting together extensive dossiers on people who are so secretive that their names have never even appeared in the *Times* or any other paper.

Saul gets at least double the going day-rate for free-lancers and still rejects more work than he accepts, but he almost never turns Wolfe down. And he never turns down a chance to take *my* money, either, in our weekly poker games.

" 'Morning," I said when he answered on the second ring. "I thought you'd be out combing the streets of this great metropolis by now."

"As a matter of fact, I was just about to leave. An interesting situation over in Long Island City, should wrap it up today. What can I do you out of?"

"You did me out of enough with that flush against my jack-high straight the other night. I'm just casting for some information."

"Cast away."

"What can you tell me about Sparky Linville?"

"Oh, yeah . . . the hotshot with the heavy foot, the one who got pinched going one-fifteen on the Grand Central Parkway in a Porsche a couple weeks ago. You probably read about it."

"Keep going."

"Hell, Archie, you see the papers. You know as much as I do. The punk's got money backing up on him. And women too, apparently. The spoiled-prince syndrome, you know?"

"Into drugs?"

"Possibly, but I haven't heard anything specific. Then, there's no reason I should. Linville and I don't exactly move in the same circles."

"Where does he live?"

"I haven't the foggiest. Say, what's your interest in the young rake, anyway?"

"I'm enamored of his life-style, as in rich and famous, and I want to learn to be just like him."

"Why do I not believe you?" Saul muttered. "Okay, let me get back to you. Going anywhere in the next few minutes?"

"Only as far from the telephone as my faithful PC. You got a pipeline?"

My answer was the click followed by the dial tone, so I swiveled to the computer and began entering the germination records from the three-by-five cards Theodore had left on my desk the night before. I was at it for every bit of six minutes when the phone squawked. "Got a writing implement handy?" Saul asked.

"Of course. What took you so long?"

"Mr. Linville," he said, ignoring the sarcasm, "is the product of what the historians would refer to as a dynastic marriage. His given name is Barton, which is his mother's maiden name. As in the department-store Bartons: And his father, as you probably know, owns most of Linville Frozen Foods. The heir, an only child, is twenty-six, and he lives alone—at least most of the time—in a pricey three-bedroom pleasure dome in what was described to me as an old but elegant co-op on East Seventy-seventh." He gave me the address. "His favorite nocturnal haunt is, surprise, surprise, that yuppie playpen, Morgana's, which he hits at least two or three times a week, frequently in the company of at least one well-turned-out young female, sometimes two, other times with a date and another couple or with one or more male friends. Being a classy fellow, he's also been known to thump his chest and bellow about his amorous conquests. And in case you didn't know it, Morgana's, or so I'm told, is an overpriced chrome-and-glass temple on Second Avenue frequented by a well-cushioned crowd ranging from their twenties upward who want to be talked about and written about and seen, mostly by one another."

"It may shock you, but I've been there."

"Very little shocks me," Saul said, "although that comes close."

"I like to be unpredictable. Anyway, I gather what you're telling me is that our Mr. Linville eschews the solitary and contemplative life."

"Don't ever let anybody ever say you don't have a way with the mother tongue," Saul shot back. "I couldn't have put it better myself. Anyway, if you're still with me on this, our hero has been known to favor Morgana's with his presence for up to three hours at a stretch, usually middle-to-late evening, and then sometimes he moves off with his entourage to one of several places in the Village or SoHo. He's described as a moderate drinker, Scotch usually, but once in a while he sails past his limit and then he tends to get a tad surly. He's not all that large, and he picked a fight in Morgana's some months back with somebody who is. Result: Young Barton Linville ended up on his keester. No major damage, except to his pride."

"You're a veritable storehouse of information. I am truly impressed."

"As well you should be. I've got more if you can take the time away from your precious PC."

"I'll make the sacrifice."

"Dandy. Our prince has a job—or at least a position—at his father's frozen-foods company. From what I gather, it's a sinecure, and he doesn't do a hell of a lot there to earn whatever money falls his way from out of the old man's pocket."

"Kid sounds like a real jewel."

"Uh-huh. Well, I've done my good deed for the day. It's off to Long Island City." Before I could thank Saul, the line had gone dead again.

I went to the shelves where we keep a month's copies of both the *Gazette* and the *Times* and took a chance on the *Gazette*, lugging three weeks' worth back to my desk. Naturally, what I was looking for was in an issue near the bottom of the stack—a photo of a grinning, tuxedoed Linville at a benefit dinner for neighborhood food pantries the night after his speeding episode on the Grand Central Parkway. The cap-

tion described him as a "free-wheeling, fun-loving dynamo-about-town" and quoted him as defending his driving thusly: "Really, what's the big deal? It's a great-handling car. And I was sober, wasn't I? I demanded a breathalizer test, and I passed—no alcohol at all, not a trace. Hell, I'm a safer driver at a hundred than most of those clowns on the road are at forty-five or fifty."

My next move was to dial Fred Durkin, a freelance operative Wolfe and I use when we can't get Saul or when we need two men or when the job doesn't call for a bushel of finesse. Fred, who stands five-ten and is a marginal Weight Watchers' candidate, is by no means a dummy, but he's a little rusty upstairs sometimes, although he has three traits—bravery, honesty, and dependability—that in Wolfe's book and mine more than compensate for whatever he might be lacking in the penthouse. I knew business had been a little slow for Fred lately, so I wasn't surprised to find him at home in Queens at a time when most people are pursuing an income.

"Mr. Wolfe have a job?" he blurted before I could finish my sentence of pleasantries.

"Not Mr. Wolfe—me. It's a stakeout, at your usual rates, of course."

"Fire away. I'm available, like right now."

"Tonight's soon enough, although this could take more than one night."

I filled him in on the program. He didn't recall ever having heard of Linville, but he did know where Morgana's was. We agreed that he would stop by the brownstone to get the *Gazette* photo before six, which is when Wolfe comes down from his afternoon session in the plant rooms. Fred has always been a little uncomfortable around Wolfe. Besides, this time around, he was working for me, not Wolfe, and what I do on my own time is nobody's business but my own.

THREE

I was once told by a guest in the brownstone, a steel-company executive by the name of Hazlitt, who was a client of ours, that dining with Nero Wolfe is a singular event. I have no doubt Mr. Hazlitt knew whereof he spoke, although I'm the least-qualified person on the planet to respond to that comment, having sat at the same table with His Largeness so often over the years that I may fail to totally appreciate what others experience when they make a debut visit to our dining room.

Our normal routine—which is to say something over ninety-nine percent of the time—calls for both lunch and dinner to be served in the dining room, which is across the hall from the office on the first floor. Fritz does the serving, and Wolfe and I are usually the only servees, although on occasion, guests such as Mr. Hazlitt are invited by Wolfe to join us. Tonight, though, it was just the two of us, and Wolfe had set the discussion topic, which also is part of the routine.

As we laid waste to the lamb-cutlet casserole with tomatoes and carrots, he expounded on why the Roman Empire was doomed from its inception, and I mostly nodded and chewed, throwing in an occasional question to show that I was listening and interested. The casserole was easily up to Fritz's five-star standards, as was the peach cobbler that chased it. When we were back in the office with coffee, Wolfe immediately burrowed into his current book, *Louis XIV: A Royal Life,* by Olivier Bernier, which pleased me if only because it gave me time to reflect on how I would approach Sparky Linville if Fred chanced to call. I can't claim my reflective moods come all that often, but when they do, it's nice to have Wolfe otherwise occupied.

After forty-five minutes of drinking coffee and watching Wolfe turn pages, I rolled my chair over to the PC to massage the orchid-germination records I'd entered earlier. No sooner had I settled in than the phone rang, and answering it is part of my unwritten job description. "Nero Wolfe's office, Archie Goodwin speaking."

"Fred. Subject just entered Morgana's, with another male. I'm across the street in the doorway of a poster shop. I'll wait here in case subject flies. Instructions?"

"Sounds good. Thanks." I hung up, convinced that the lack of work was causing Fred Durkin to watch too many TV police shows. His dialogue needed work. I waited five minutes, then got up and stretched, yawning.

"Think I'll take a stroll," I told Wolfe. "I could use the exercise, and the weather's on my side."

"Indeed?" he said, raising his eyebrows, setting his book down, and ringing for beer. "Who was on the telephone?"

"Fred, to tell me he can make our next poker game. See you later." I didn't get an answer, but then, I didn't expect one. As I walked out of the office, I looked back and saw that Wolfe had returned to his book.

When I'm working on a case, I'll sometimes take a taxi, sometimes the Mercedes sedan that Wolfe owns and I drive. But because this was me operating on my own, there was no question as to transportation. After leaving the brownstone and making sure that Fritz had bolted the door behind me, I walked east on

Thirty-fifth in the cool, pleasant air and after six minutes of waving my arms flagged a cab on Eighth Avenue, telling him to let me off on the corner half a block from Morgana's.

Traffic was relatively light, both on the streets and the sidewalks, and it wasn't hard to spot Fred when the hack dropped me off on Second Avenue. He was standing in front of a poster shop that had closed for the night, and he looked about as inconspicuous as a leopard in a Laundromat.

"How nice to see a friendly face," I said as I walked up to him, wondering if I should have spent the extra dollars to hire Saul.

"Archie, unless there's a back way, which I can't believe, he's in there," Fred hissed in a voice just above a whisper, even though no one was within a grenade's throw of us. "I haven't been out of sight of the entrance since I called you. He came up in a cab with another young guy. I recognized Linville right off from the photo. He's fairly short—I'd put him at five-eight. Dark, shiny hair. He's wearing a light brown sport coat, a dark sport shirt, no tie, tan pants. The guy he's with has light hair, almost white, and he's even shorter than Linville, I mean, *really* short, like five-three or four, if that. He's got on a blue blazer, gray slacks, open-collared white shirt."

"Thanks," I said, feeling vaguely ashamed of my earlier doubts. "Okay, I'll take it from here." I peeled off bills that easily covered his time and held them out.

"I can wait," he said stiffly. "Except for expenses, Mr. Wolfe always pays me by check. You know that—you're the one who writes them."

"Right," I said, jamming the greenbacks into my pocket. "I just thought—"

"You just thought *what?*" Fred fired back, breaking out of his near-whisper. "That maybe I was hard up? That I'm a charity case? Forget it!" He stalked off down the street.

I called after him but got no response, and he disappeared into the darkness. So far, my record as an employer was enough to suggest I could take lessons from Wolfe, hard as I found that to accept. I vowed to patch things up with Fred tomorrow, then shifted my attention to the opposite side of the street.

Morgana's was not totally alien to me; I'd been there once—which was plenty. That was with Lily a half-dozen years ago, when the place was considered "hot" by whoever does the considering. We had gone with some friends of hers after a charity dinner, and what sticks in my mind is how much the owners must have spent on chrome and etched glass and spotlights and metallic wallpaper.

The clientele, which I recalled from that night as ranging from young and pleased with themselves to young-middle-aged and even more pleased with themselves, seemed mostly bored, both with each other and with the surroundings. And I distinctly recall that my Scotch and water was markedly light on Scotch.

As for the dancing—ha! Okay, it was a disco, plain and simple, but that didn't stop Lily and me from giving the assemblage a few of our moves out on the floor. We may not be Astaire and Rogers—quite— but I like to think the young pups and even the lounge lizards picked up a little something from us that night.

So much for the stroll down memory lane. Morgana's is in a nondescript five-story brick apartment building in a nondescript block of Second Avenue in the Seventies. In keeping with its neo-Babylonian interior, somebody concluded chrome-look double doors were the answer to the entrance and then went a step further by framing the doors in something that looked like pink marble and topped the whole business off with a lavender canopy trimmed in pink fringe.

Why they chose to outfit the doorman in light blue escaped me, but then, I never passed the design-school entrance exams. I briefly considered going inside; after all, the place isn't really a private club—it just acts like it is. But I vetoed that course of action because I preferred to make the acquaintance of Sparky Linville in the relative peace and quiet of Second Avenue, rather than the hubbub of the disco. I leaned against the metal grillwork that had been pulled down over the windows of the poster shop and waited.

Actually, I was glad for the doorman, regardless of his garb, because he was the only sign of life at Morgana's for the first seventeen minutes I kept watch. Oh, there were passersby, all right, including a bag lady who turned to smile at me and comment on the nice weather and a gray-haired jogger wearing shorts and a T-shirt advertising an FM radio station who almost ran me down on the sidewalk, probably because he was preoccupied by whatever was assaulting his senses through his headphones.

Anyway, Morgana's was hardly hopping, unless, contrary to Fred's observation, there was indeed a back door through which hordes of eager visitors were funneling. Finally a cab delivered one young couple, then another, and a third twosome, not quite as young, departed and the doorman listlessly flagged a taxi for them. I yawned, half-wishing I still smoked, and leaned back, trying to find a way to get comfortable with a metal grille as a vertical mattress. The luminous dial on my watch told me it was ten-twenty. Was it possible that Sparky Linville had found a reason to spend the whole night in Morgana's?

Just when I was beginning to seriously consider packing it in, the chrome doors swung open and out popped the subject himself, along with his sidekick. Before I continue, honesty compels me to report that when, the next morning, I filled Wolfe in on the events at Morgana's, he was understandably less than impressed. "Archie," he said, "as I have stated often, your impetuosity constitutes both a signal strength and a glaring liability. This episode manifestly demonstrates the latter. You were without a feasible plan."

Okay, so Wolfe had it right. I hadn't used those so-called reflective moments back in the office to plan anything remotely resembling a strategy. Anyway, these two guys were out on the sidewalk in front of Morgana's talking to the doorman as I hustled across the street, dodging a car and a Korean delivery boy on his bike. The doorman had his lips puckered to use his cab whistle when I joined the threesome. "Sparky Linville?" I said to the taller one, who had slicked-back dark hair and deep-set, brooding eyes that made him seem as if he'd just stepped out of a Giorgio Armani magazine ad.

Linville turned toward me and gave a tense Kirk Douglas smile, showing a perfect set of pearlies. "Could be. What's it to ya, Jack?" So far, he seemed to be in character.

"I want to talk to you for a few minutes—alone." I looked meaningfully at his sawed-off, white-headed friend and then at the doorman. The latter seemed to be exceedingly interested in the buttons on his powder-blue coat.

"And just what have we got here, yet another newspaperman?" Linville folded his arms across his chest and tilted his head to one side, chin up. "I haven't seen you before, have I now, old chap?" he said. I know Lexington Avenue hot-dog vendors who can do a better English accent.

"No, I'm not with a paper, I—"

Linville's pipsqueak friend cut in with a word I'm not going to repeat on these pages, but which got my attention. "Listen, you pygmy weasel, how'd you like to be used as a street sweeper?" I said, pivoting toward him. He repeated the word, and reflexively I cocked my right arm, but it was halted by the doorman before I could start its arc, which was just as well. At that moment, a well-dressed yuppie couple emerged from Morgana's, and the woman, wearing a white fur jacket that was superfluous given the weather, let out a squeal. "Oh, Josh, they're fighting," she keened in a liquor-laced tone. "How awful!"

"How *stupid*, you mean," Josh huffed in a voice that showed one member of the pair to be sober, even if he didn't know how to match a sport coat and slacks. "This place started going downhill months ago. Damned if we'll be back. Come on, we can find our own cab."

"Please, sir, I'm going to have to ask you to move on. I know you don't want any trouble," the doorman said quietly, his hand gripping my wrist. He was probably pushing sixty, with white hair, a red face, and blue eyes that matched his silly coat, and he looked at me with a long-suffering expression, as if he'd seen it all right out here in front of Morgana's and it had stopped holding his interest a generation ago.

"Yeah, listen to the man and stir the dust, Jack," young Linville said, shedding his lamentable English accent, "or I'll lose my patience and turn Hallie here loose on you."

The shrimps both guffawed, and the doorman, whom I could easily have brushed aside and who knew it, gradually released his hold on my wrist. "Please, sir," he repeated, "I'll have to ask you to leave these gentlemen alone."

"You need to work on your terminology," I said evenly, but we all knew I had lost the skirmish. As I turned and stalked off, the laughter of the two followed me, along with the shrill of the doorman's cab whistle.

FOUR

I've never been much for saloon drinking, particularly when I'm alone, but I made an exception that night. After leaving the trio in front of Morgana's, I walked south on Second Avenue for about six blocks. I was still steaming when I decided to drop into a small Irish bar that wasn't doing much business. Two Scotch-and-waters later, I was still plenty mad, but at least I was beginning to unwind and not think about the satisfaction it would give me to drop-kick both Linville and his gutter-mouthed little buddy off the Fifty-ninth Street Bridge into the East River.

Even with the relaxed feeling the drinks gave me, I felt my system could benefit from more exercise, so I tipped the bartender and walked the rest of the way home, arriving on the front stoop of the brownstone at twelve-seventeen. Because the door was double-locked, I had to ring for Fritz to let me in, which didn't make me feel guilty because he always stays up reading till well past midnight. Wolfe had turned in, though, I noticed as I peeked into the dark office on my way up to bed.

Despite the turmoil of the evening, I slept hard, getting my quota, and was in the kitchen at the usual time the next morning with the *Times*, coffee, wheatcakes delivered to me one at a time hot off the griddle by Fritz, and all the other wonderful things he shovels my way for breakfast. While I read, one corner of my mind kept gnawing away at a strategy for tackling

Linville again. As far as I was concerned, one round does not a fight make.

I was still thinking about Round Two in the office at a quarter to nine when the phone rang.

"Archie!" It was Lily, in a voice that sounded like she wasn't getting enough oxygen.

"What is it—you all right?"

"Archie, did you see . . . *him* last night?"

"Linville? Yeah, but the less said about that, the better. I'm afraid that I didn't exactly cover myself with glory, although— "

"Archie—he's *dead!*"

"Wha-a-a-t? Are you talking about Sparky Linville?"

"Yes." Her voice was a whisper. "Dead. Killed. In a parking garage. Last night. I . . . ."

"Hey, stay with me on this," I said. "First, it wasn't me, if that's on your mind. Although I confess that the idea isn't exactly a repugnant one, particularly after having met him. Tell me what you know."

"I just heard it on the radio. I had the news on and . . . he's dead."

"How?"

"They said he was found early this morning in the garage where he keeps his car. He was . . . hit over the head with something, I don't think they said what."

"And this was on the radio?"

"Yes, one of the all-news stations. I usually listen while I do my hair. God, Archie, what happened, did you—?"

"Hey, easy. I told you it wasn't me. I saw him, yes, in front of Morgana's, along with a foul-mouthed pal he called Hallie. Words got exchanged, that's all, and damn few of them at that. Was there any more in the radio report?"

"Not much," Lily said. Her voice was gradually returning to normal. "A garage attendant found him lying on the concrete next to his car. Apparently it was well into the wee hours."

"Which would explain why it wasn't in the *Times*. All right, I've got some calls to make; I'll keep you posted. But before I go, it would be nice to know that you believe me."

"Oh, of course I do." She didn't hesitate for a second, bless her. "It's just that it seems so strange that the day after we talked about this . . ."

"I know, I know. It would appear that someone else had reason to harbor animus toward the junior Mr. Linville."

We said good-bye and I was about to dial Lon Cohen at the *Gazette* when the doorbell rang. I knew Fritz was out marketing so I went to the front hall and peeked through the one-way panel in the door. What I saw was none other than Fred Durkin, wearing a worried expression and a tie that was old enough to remember when the Weehawken ferry still ran.

"I haven't seen you in all of twelve hours," I said, pulling the door open. "Come on in."

He muttered his thanks, studying his knuckles. "Archie, about last night, I—"

"Come on into the office," I told him, "where we can sit. Want some coffee?"

Fred shook his head and followed me, taking one of the yellow chairs while I parked at my desk. He looked down at his hands again and cleared his throat twice. "I'm sorry about getting sore last night," he muttered, shaking his head some more.

I grinned. "Not to worry. We've been friends long enough to tolerate each other's moods."

"Aw, there was no excuse for my getting hot. The fact is, Archie, I *am* hurting for work, and I guess I've gotten a little bit touchy about it. That's no reason for me to take it out on you, though."

"Consider it forgotten. Now, while you're here, will you accept a check for last night?"

"Sure," he said, smiling sheepishly.

I got my own checkbook out and wrote out a figure equal to what Fred would have gotten from

Wolfe for the same amount of time. "By the way," I said, "have you heard the radio or TV news this morning?" He shook his head.

"Well, it seems that the subject of our surveillance last night got himself put to sleep—permanently."

"Killed?"

"Very. It'll be all over the papers by this afternoon. I don't know much yet. But it's just possible that before this is over, your services may be needed again."

Fred stood up, looking puzzled, and absently took the check I held out. "I'll help any way I can," he said. "Are you in trouble, Archie?"

I laughed. "No. But you're the second person this morning who's thought that."

Back at my desk after letting Fred out, I called Lon Cohen.

Lon doesn't have an official title I'm aware of at the New York *Gazette*, but his office is within a horseshoe pitch of the publisher's, and he seems to know the skinny about everything that happens in New York, from scandals in high places to false fire alarms on Staten Island. And best of all, Lon is a friend; his information has been invaluable to Wolfe and me on cases, and conversely, we've been able to repay him with scoops worthy of headlines.

He answered on the first ring. "What's going on?" he yapped in his usual "I-have-seven-seconds-to-spare" tone.

"Just wondering what you've got on the Linville murder."

"How in the hell does that one interest you?"

"I'm not entirely sure," I told him. "And what's more, I'm not even sure that if it does end up interesting me, I'll even be able to tell you why."

"Just what I like—cooperative friends of the media," Lon groused. "Okay, I'll shovel it to you fast: Barton David Linville, aka Sparky, age twenty-six, heir to something in the neighborhood of six million simoleons, was found dead at approximately four-thirty this morning by the attendant in the Mark 2 parking garage on East Seventy-seventh Street. Linville was lying on the concrete next to his car, this year's model Porsche. His skull had been crushed. No weapon was found. The police think he could have been bashed by a tire iron, or maybe a wrench, but it really sounds like they're guessing on that."

"Suspects?"

"Not that we've heard of yet. The kid was a wild one, drove his car like he was on the track at Indy, had plenty of women around, got into a few bar fights, nothing serious that I can recall, though."

"That's it?"

"What do you want for nothing? The body was discovered only four and a half hours ago. Your time is up—I gotta run."

I hadn't been off the phone with Lon for more than fifteen seconds when it rang again, and I knew who it was before I lifted the receiver.

"Is what I just heard on the radio simply one of those incredible coincidences, the kind the *Reader's Digest* sometimes writes about?" Saul Panzer asked.

"You don't even get the *Reader's Digest,*" I said.

"Don't evade the question."

"Yes, it really *is* a coincidence. It's possible I'll tell you about it sometime. It's also possible I won't."

"Ever the enigma. Okay, Archie, if you need any help, you have the number."

I told him it was appreciated and leaned back in my chair, contemplating the rows of bookshelves on the far wall of the office. Wolfe wouldn't be down from his morning session with the plants for another hundred minutes, which gave me time to think about how I was going to drop all this on him. I was still thinking about it at two minutes after eleven, when the whir of the elevator told me he was descending from his greenhouse in the sky.

"Good morning, Archie. Did you sleep well?" That

was his standard opening question, and I gave him my standard affirmative answer as he detoured around his desk and got his bulk settled in the best-reinforced chair in North America. He rang for beer and shuffled through the morning mail, which I had as usual stacked neatly on the blotter. He then read and signed three letters that I'd typed while meditating on how to approach him. I waited until he had set them aside and poured beer into a glass from one of the two chilled bottles Fritz had brought.

"We need to talk," I said.

"Indeed?" He raised his eyebrows and leaned back, lacing his fingers over his center mound, a feat you have to see to believe.

"Yeah, indeed. I'm breaking a confidence, but you don't count. As you've said yourself, on matters of business, we are as one. I'm not sure that what I'm going to tell you will ever grow into a business matter for us, but as far as I'm concerned, it's close enough. If that's what you call a rationalization, so be it."

"Continue," Wolfe said, his eyes closed. With that, I laid it all out in detail, from a verbatim report of my talk with Lily right through to the events of the morning, including Fred's visit and my phone conversations with Lily, Lon, and Saul.

Wolfe alternately scowled, frowned, and drank beer, and also injected an occasional question or comment, including the remark I mentioned earlier about my impetuosity. "You know I view you to have better-than-adequate percipience," he said when I had finished. "What do you feel the likelihood is that either Mr. Linville's friend or the doorman could identify you?"

"That's a tough one," I said. "At the risk of appearing immodest, I *am* somewhat well-known, if only because of my long association with you. And you, as everyone knows, are one of New York's 'One Hundred Most Interesting People,' as selected by *Big Apple* magazine."

FIVE

Wolfe's scowl deepened when he learned who our visitor was. "Confound it, show him in," he sighed, putting on one of his long-suffering expressions. Despite what he has said in the past about the relationship between host and guest being sacred, he has been known to make exceptions—Inspector Cramer of the New York Police Department's Homicide Bureau notable among them. I won't go so far as to say that Wolfe and Cramer flat out don't like each other—actually, I think each of them secretly enjoys verbally sniping at the other. Heaven knows they've had enough practice through the years. But Cramer's trips to the brownstone usually end with him storming out, which is upsetting to Wolfe's sense of order and decorum—never mind that he is almost invariably the cause of the storming.

"Good morning, Inspector," I said with a smile after swinging open the front door. "To what do we we the unexpected pleasure?"

That got me a glare and more as Cramer, his road face a trifle ruddier than usual, stomped into the front hall. "You ..." He bit off whatever comment he had prepared, waggled a finger, shook his head, and barreled into the office ahead of me.

As he has so many times before, the inspector eelined to the red leather chair, not waiting for an vitation to be seated. His bulk, which would have

That brought a new scowl, which was still Wolfe's face when the doorbell rang a few secon later. For the second time that morning, I went to hall to look through the one-way panel. This tir however, I returned to the office without opening door to our visitor.

"I think your question about my being identi has been answered," I said to Wolfe. "Planted on stoop—and looking far from overjoyed to be the might add—is none other than Inspector Cramer been impressive in any context but this, made the cushion wheeze on contact.

"Well?" he spat at Wolfe, taking a cigar from his breast pocket and jamming it unlit into his mouth. Cramer uses stogies the way most people use chewing gum.

"Well indeed?" Wolfe responded. "We have not seen each other for some months, sir. Have you been well?"

"Can the solicitousness!" Cramer snarled. "I think you know why I'm here."

"Think again, Mr. Cramer. And enlighten us, please, since you went to the trouble of coming. Will you have something to drink?" To Wolfe, anyone voluntarily voyaging into the outside world qualifies as a latter-day Marco Polo—intrepid, fearless, and of questionable mental stability.

Cramer took a deep breath and a nasty bite out of his cigar and leaned forward, palms on knees. "No thanks on the drink," he said gruffly. "All right, I'll play this like you don't know anything, even though I refuse to believe that for a second. Last night, this morning, actually, a kid—if you want to call some-body who's twenty-six a kid—was murdered in a ga-rage on the Upper East Side. His name was Barton Linville. Maybe you've heard of him."

Wolfe nodded for Cramer to go on.

"He was found by an attendant on the floor of the garage next to his car, a Porsche. One side of his head—the left—was pretty well caved in. Cause of death, mas-sive head injuries, from a blow or a series of blows. Time of death, estimated at between midnight and one. His watch crystal was shattered, but the watch was still running, so that's as close as we can come to an exact time. The body had no bullet wounds or other indications of violence. No weapon has been found."

Wolfe leaned back in his chair. "And you come here seeking advice?" he asked.

"I'm not done!" Cramer barked. "In the first place, this Linville kid, they called him Sparky, comes

from money on both sides—frozen foods and department stores—which means there's a lot of heat being
generated, and which I'm sure you don't give a fig
about. Anyway, we've been checking into his activities
of last night, and we found something interesting."
Cramer paused to study Wolfe, maybe expecting a
reaction, but he didn't get even raised eyebrows for
his theatrics.

"We talked to another kid that Linville had spent
a good part of the evening with—a guy named Todd
Halliburton, who's apparently an old friend. Anyway,
this Halliburton says that when the two of them were
walking out of a nightspot on Second Avenue, a place
called Morgana's, some guy tried to give Linville a
hard time out in front on the sidewalk. And who do
you suppose that guy was?"

"Mr. Cramer," Wolfe said, rearranging his bulk,
"if you have ventured forth to assault me with guessing games, you risk the immediate loss of an audience. I suggest that you forgo your charade and come
to the point."

Cramer's face took on a decidedly unhealthy shade
of plum. "Charade, eh? You're damn right I'll come
to the point. The man on the sidewalk who hassled
Linville is in this room."

Wolfe finished his beer and set the empty glass
down deliberately, dabbing his lips with one of the
fresh handkerchiefs Fritz puts in his center desk drawer
every morning. "Really, sir," he said, "are you suggesting that I have taken to nocturnal wanderings and
hostile confrontations on street corners?"

"You're getting as bad as Goodwin with the smart
remarks," Cramer shot back. "When we talked to
Halliburton, and that was only an hour ago, he said
Goodwin came up to them outside Morgana's and
seemed like he was looking for a scrap with Linville.
Halliburton said he recognized Goodwin from pictures he'd seen of him in the papers. Heaven knows
you've both had your mugs in print often enough.

Care to comment?" Cramer looked at me and back at Wolfe, then glared at his cigar as if wondering how it had traveled from his mouth to his hand.

"Sir, are you in the habit of accepting identifications like Mr. Halliburton's without attempting to verify them?" Wolfe asked dryly.

Cramer leaned forward, sticking his chin out. "Of course not, and you know it. But since you asked, we pulled some glossy eight-by-tens of about five of our lieutenants, in civilian clothes, along with a similar shot of Goodwin from my file on him—it's a dupe of the one he turned in with his last license renewal. Anyway, we showed them all to Halliburton and he pointed to Goodwin instantly. He was emphatic about it."

"Inspector, I'm touched that you have a file on me," I said, grinning.

"Yeah. It's mainly filled with press clippings about you and Wolfe, most of them due to your personal publicist, Cohen. I keep them around to read when I need inspiration."

I thought for sure Wolfe would use that line as an opening to zing Cramer, but he just scowled. "Mr. Cramer, are you suggesting that Mr. Goodwin is in some way implicated in this young man's demise?"

"You're damn right I am! And what you once referred to as my native cynicism forces me to ask three questions: One, was that in fact Goodwin trading words with Linville in front of the fleshpot? Two, if yes, why? And three, where was he between midnight and dawn?"

"Well, Archie, do you care to respond?" Wolfe asked, raising his eyebrows.

"Sure, why not? Answer to number one—yes. To number two—I'm not at liberty to say at this time, maybe never. And to number three—upstairs in my room dreaming about a World Series between the Mets and Yankees that the Mets sweep in four straight, all shutouts, including a no-hitter by Gooden. By the way, Fritz let me in at precisely seventeen minutes after the witching hour. If Mr. Wolfe doesn't have any objections, you can check with him."

"Just what I need—a disinterested party like your pal Brenner supplying your alibi."

"Take it or leave it; I was just trying to be helpful."

"Balls!" Cramer bellowed. "If you're so damn helpful, what's to hide about your connection with Linville?"

"Sir, I think we have been more than indulgent," Wolfe injected. "You show no connection between their conflux on the sidewalk and Mr. Linville's violent death a few hours later—and indeed, there is none."

"So I should chalk all this up to coincidence, is that it?" Cramer had done a number on the poor stogie and looked like he was about to start chewing the corner of Wolfe's desk.

Wolfe raised his shoulders and let them drop. "How you respond is your business."

"Why is it that whenever there's a big case in this town, particularly one that generates publicity, you two are somehow hip-deep in it?" Cramer rasped, pushing himself to his feet.

"Just lucky, I guess," I remarked.

"Listen," Cramer roared, jabbing a thick index finger in Wolfe's direction, "with what's happened, we can make things hot for Goodwin, as in blast-furnace hot. You're so goddamn smug, both of you—well, let's see who ends up laughing." He flung what was left of the cigar at the wastebasket, missing as usual. I used to think his aim was lousy, but in the last few years I think I've finally figured it out: He's always so mad and so frustrated after a visit to the brownstone that cigar-littering is his endearing way of getting some revenge.

By the time I got to my feet, Cramer, who moves remarkably well for a big man, already was in the hall. I was a full three paces behind him when he pulled open the front door, turning to me with a final salvo.

"One way or another, Goodwin, there's a good chance you could find yourself getting bloodied on this one—and Wolfe too. And if that should happen, by God, I can't say it will bother me one bit." Before I could reach the door, Cramer had slammed it behind him so hard that the small picture of the windmill next to the coatrack rattled and slipped to a cockeyed angle. I straightened it and went back to the office. "The man seemed a touch out of sorts," I said to Wolfe.

"Archie, you enjoy quoting odds," he said quietly as he reached for his book. "This time, however, I cast myself in the role of bookmaker. I shall give fifteen-to-one that we have not heard the last of this affair."

"Funny, that's essentially what Cramer communicated as he left, although in somewhat less genteel terms," I replied. "Anyway, it's no bet. Right now, I wouldn't take twenty-five-to-one, and you know how much I enjoy betting on long shots."

SIX

It didn't take even twenty-four hours to prove
Wolfe a good oddsmaker, but then, I'm getting ahead of myself. I knew the afternoon edition of
the *Gazette* would play Linville's murder big, and Lon
didn't disappoint me. The banner was WEALTHY HEIR
SLAIN, accompanied by a news story that jumped to
page two, a head-and-shoulders photo of a grinning
Linville in black tie, a picture of the murder scene, i.e.,
the concrete floor of an Upper East Side garage, and
both a related story and a lead editorial on how neither poor nor rich are safe in an age of mindless
violence. Friday morning's *Times*, which I read as I ate
breakfast, was more subdued, but it also gave the
killing plenty of play, beginning with a front-page
story under a two-column headline and Linville's
picture—almost identical to the one the *Gazette* used.

Back to Wolfe's oddsmaking. On Friday morning
at a little past nine, having digested both breakfast
and *Times*, I was in the office fiddling with the orchid-
germination records on the PC when I got a call from
one very upset Lily Rowan.

"Archie, the police are holding Noreen's brother,
and Megan's ranting, and—"

"Slow down, you're already five laps ahead of me.
Now tell me exactly what—wait a second, maybe it
would make more sense if I came over. How does that
sound?"

Lily, catching her breath, allowed as to how that

seemed like a good idea, which is why I was in her apartment less than fifteen minutes later and one New York cabbie had a fifty-percent tip. I was parked on a sofa in the living room when she came in, looking a lot less composed than usual.

"Okay," I said before she could begin, "take it from the top, and go slowly, for my benefit. First, I gather the cops have your nephew—Michael, isn't that his name?"

She nodded, sucking in her cheeks. "I got a call from Megan right before I talked to you. If you thought *I* was a little unhinged when I phoned you, you should have heard her; she was just this side of hysterical. It took me several minutes to get things straight, but it seems it's all out in the open now that Sparky Linville had attacked Noreen. Apparently Megan wormed it out of her shortly after she got home from that European trip. Anyway, what I was able to learn is that—"

Lily stopped because the phone on the end table next to her was squawking. "It's Megan again," she said, cupping the receiver. "I think I'd better go over there. Would you be willing to come along?"

I nodded.

"Megan, Archie is with me. I'd like to bring him . . . Yes, I know . . . but first off, he's the most discreet person I know, and second, he's used to dealing with the police. He . . . no, of *course* he's not going to run to the newspapers or TV." She looked at me and rolled her beautiful eyes. "Yes . . . uh-huh . . . yes, Megan. Yes. All right. We'll get there as fast as we can."

"So," she said, cradling the receiver with a soft sigh, "my dear half-sister is still just this side of hysteria, but at least she has the good sense to want me there to provide something resembling stability. Aided by your soothing presence, of course."

"It was apparent she was ecstatic with that idea."

"Oh, stop being so sensitive. She'll learn soon

enough that to know you is to love you. And besides, at this point, she'd agree to anything."

"Thanks for that ringing endorsement," I said with what I hoped was a sardonic grin as we headed for the door and a taxi.

I had never been in the James apartment, which Lily had once described to me as "Art Deco run rampant." And as partial as I am to Deco, I was unprepared for what greeted me as we got off the elevator on the sixth floor of an ordinary brick building in the East Eighties. The oval-shaped foyer had walls of vertically fluted black marble with a white Roman-style settee, two chrome-framed floor-to-ceiling mirrors, and six silver sunburst light sconces, not to mention the indirect lighting tucked into the ceiling moldings.

"You ain't seen nothing yet, pal," Lily put in. "And remember, her Xanadu taketh the whole floor, as in eleven rooms." Just then the door, done in the same silver pattern as the light fixtures, swung open, revealing a small olive-skinned, black-haired woman in a maid's get-up. "Hello, Carmella," Lily said with a smile.

Carmella smiled back, dipped ever so slightly in what looked suspiciously like a curtsy, and ushered us into an entrance hall that would have worked just fine as the lobby of one of the smaller Rockefeller Center buildings. We passed through that into a drawing room that looked as if it were the set for the Thin Man movies, except that in Myrna Loy's place was Megan James, standing grimly behind a peach-colored tuxedo-style sofa that could have seated the entire Mets' pitching staff. And instead of William Powell, over at the small bar in the corner was a guy in a dandy brown three-piece suit with chiseled features and graying hair who looked like he belonged in the House of Lords—or at the very least in a magazine ad for premium whiskey.

"Hello, Megan. I think you remember Archie Goodwin," Lily said as we went in.

"I do," her semi-sister answered coolly, stepping around the sofa but not offering a hand. She was wearing a dark blue belted dress that whispered its elegance. "I suppose I should thank you for coming along. This is my friend Edward Pamsett. Edward, I think you've met Lily before. And this is Mr. Goodwin."

"Miss Rowan, nice to see you again. And Mr. Goodwin," Pamsett said, smiling, bowing slightly, and holding out a paw, which each of us shook. He had a firm grip to go with his good manners, which was a point in his favor.

Megan looked like I remembered her: thin all around—body, arms, face. Actually, she might have been attractive if she ever loosened up, but everything about her was tight and taut—the dark hair skinned back to a bun, the tight lips, the look of disapproval that had permanently taken residence on a face otherwise nicely arranged. She offhandedly gestured us to sit, and within seconds Carmella had reappeared with coffee on a silver tray, which both Lily and I accepted.

"Please, bring us up-to-date," Lily said to Megan, who was still standing.

"Where do I start?" she intoned, fumbling for a cigarette, which Pamsett lit smoothly. "You know part of it, of course, from my call. When I got back from Antibes, the kids and Edward had a little welcome-back surprise party for me here, and I immediately knew by the way she looked that something was wrong with Noreen. Lord above, I hardly had to be a genius to see that. She . . . Mr. Goodwin, I know how good a friend of Lily's you are, and I'm sure she's told you at least something of what this is all about. I ask you—I beg you—to respect our privacy in this matter. As you can appreciate, this is sensitive, and very, very painful, to our whole family."

"Begging isn't necessary," I told her, struggling

to keep the irritation out of my voice. "As I think Lily said to you on the phone, I am the essence of discretion."

Megan took a couple of jerky drags on her cigarette and ground it out in a square black onyx ashtray that probably weighed as much as a bowling ball. "Yes, of course," she said without conviction. "Anyway, when I took her aside, Noreen came apart and told me about that . . . Linville situation. Needless to say, it made her very upset—probably with me as much as anything else. It was then that I found out she'd already talked to you about it," she said to Lily. "I'm glad you were here to comfort her, but the whole thing made—makes—me feel pretty damn useless." She didn't bother to hide the bitterness.

"But you *were* overseas," Lily put in. "She wouldn't have wanted to ruin your trip."

"Oh, I suppose that's true, but I just wish she'd . . ." Megan's voice trailed off and she jiggled her shoulders, as if to underscore her helplessness.

"And to think it happened to *Noreen*," Pamsett put in. "There's not a nicer, finer young woman around."

"Don't be so naive, Edward," Megan snapped. "Noreen's just as bad as the rest of them. Sometimes I think three-quarters of the young women today are just dressing and acting like they're asking for—"

"Megan!" It was Lily, with sparks in her eyes.

"Well, it's true," Megan persisted. "I know that—"

It was time to redirect the conversation. "When did Noreen's brother learn about the attack?" I interrupted.

Megan, who'd just ground out a half-smoked cigarette, pulled out another one and this time lit it herself, waving away the attentive Pamsett and his gold-plated Dunhill. "The same time I did—at the party. Up until then, she had—or so I am led to believe—kept the awful thing to herself, except of course for Lily." Her tone made it clear that she was hardly delighted with the tight relationship between aunt and niece. "And now, for God's sake, Michael's being interrogated by the police and Doyle is supposedly down there trying to find out what's going on. This is a nightmare!"

Here I find the need to do some translating for the distressed Megan. The Doyle she refers to is her former husband and the father of her two children. I had met Doyle James twice, the last time close to ten years back. He and Megan got divorced aeons ago, and although I hardly know either of them, it's easy to see why their paths diverged. Doyle is free-wheeling and gregarious and unpretentious, and she is buttoned up and social-climbing. He comes from Jersey City and is what you'd have to call a self-made man; he started with a small dry cleaner somewhere over in Jersey that grew through the years—and through his efforts—into a chain that's spread all over the northern half of the state and has, or so Lily tells me, made him easily a millionaire. From here on in, I'll let Doyle speak for himself, which he is about to do.

Megan finally sat, to the relief of the rest of us, and no sooner had she sunk into the sofa than the door chimes sounded, rocketing her back to her feet. "That must be Doyle at last," she blurted, starting for the foyer, but Carmella was already on the case, and within seconds Doyle James stood in the doorway to the drawing room, surveying the tableau. When I saw him, I remembered what had made an impression on me years before: He is one of those people whose presence seems to pull the attention of everyone in a room.

In his case, it's partly scale. Doyle James is one economy-size specimen—six-four, and probably around two-thirty. But his size is only one factor, the other—and more important—being what Wolfe calls aplomb, a word that he has used, albeit grudgingly, to describe me. James had a half-smile on his square, red-cheeked face, which was framed by a thick but well-tended acre of hair that had turned almost completely white since I had last seen him.

"Megan," he said without enthusiasm, acknowledging his ex-spouse with a nod. "And Lily. Lovely Lily." He moved across the room in three long, smooth strides, kissed her on the cheek, and gave her the kind of hug that made me glad they were related, if only by a canceled marriage. "Hello, Pamsett," he added lightly, almost as an afterthought. "And . . . it's Archie Goodwin, right? Don't believe we've met since we sat in the same box with these sisters at a game at Shea nine years ago."

"You've got a good memory," I responded, accepting his handshake. "Against the Phillies. We beat them, extra innings."

"Your own memory's not so bad either," he answered, taking a cup of coffee from Carmella and nodding a thank-you in her direction. "Youngblood hit the homer that won it."

"I'm certainly glad you remember each other," Megan sniffed. "Doyle, what did you find out? What in the hell is happening down there?"

He shook his head. "I couldn't get to Michael. I tried to make some noise. Got as far as an asinine homicide lieutenant named Rowcliff, who admitted that Michael was in the building. He wouldn't let me see him, though, but said they'll probably be through talking to him sometime this morning."

"For God's sake, Doyle, it's not as though he isn't cooperating. He went down there of his own free will when they asked him to." Megan shook her head vigorously and turned toward me. "You know about these things. Don't they have to let a family member or a lawyer be there with him if we request it?"

"How old is your son?"

"Twenty-seven."

"Then as an adult, it's pretty much up to him. They surely read him the Miranda warning."

"Which is?" Megan said. She clearly doesn't watch much television.

"The standard recitation of his rights—that anything he tells them can be used against him. And also that he has the right to a lawyer while he's being questioned. It's named for a Supreme Court ruling on a case out West some years back."

"Wait a minute," Doyle put in. "That's right, what's his name—Rowcliff . . . he told me Michael had waived having a lawyer present. I was ready to call one I know."

"But of course you didn't," Megan sniffed. "God forbid you might take some kind of action, really *do* something for a change."

Doyle started to get up. "Now, just a goddamned minute—"

"I don't like the sound of this," I cut in, looking Doyle back into his seat and then turning toward Megan. "How did you find out that Michael was going in for questioning?"

Megan shot an icy look at Lily, probably to underscore her objection to the presence of yours truly. Lily smiled back serenely. "He called me from his apartment this morning—he lives over on the West Side," Megan said. "He told me a policeman was there and wanted him to go to headquarters for questioning about the Linville death. I asked him if I could do anything—phone a lawyer or whatever—and he said no. He didn't sound very concerned at all. But now that they've got him, I'll bet those bastards are keeping him from calling anyone!"

"Not likely," I told her. "This is Inspector Cramer's case, and I know him pretty well. In fact, he knew your and Lily's father years ago. He's hard as nails, and mule-headed as they come, but he's honest and fair—and smart too, despite what Mr. Wolfe may say about him at times. He'd never jeopardize a case by messing up some procedure involving rights."

"Then why is it you don't like the sound of this?"

Megan demanded, digging the thin heels of her blue Maud Frizon pumps into the plush carpet as she paced.

"I was about to ask the same thing," Pamsett said, clearing his throat and fingering his silk tie as if to call attention to it.

"For God's sake, shut up and let Goodwin say something," Doyle snarled, hammering on the end table with a meaty fist.

I ignored the crossfire. "Do any of you have any idea how the police connected Michael with Linville's death? Do they know about the episode between Linville and your daughter?"

"Not that I'm aware," Doyle said, shaking his head. "But then, I'm not what you'd call a regular fixture around here, you understand." He shot a glance at Pamsett, who tilted his aristocratic chin in what probably was meant to be indifference. "What about you, Megan?" Doyle rasped.

"I hardly would have told them, now, would I?" she snapped, studying her long crimson nails and an emerald ring the size of Connecticut. "God, it's bad enough that this many people know about it without bringing more in."

"With the attention Linville's murder is getting in the media, and is going to continue getting, chances are the publicity's just beginning," I said. "You'd better brace yourselves for more."

"That's just great, terrific, a goddamn media circus in the making." Megan ground her second cigarette into a crystal ashtray. "I suppose—"

"Instead of worrying about publicity, you'd better start worrying about Michael," Doyle James barked, glaring at her. "And I thought people were supposed to mellow with age. Goodwin, let's get back to your earlier comment, about not liking the sound of things. Explain, please."

I took a sip of coffee and was about to start in when the phone rang. Pamsett was closest to it, but

Megan darted over and waved him off, seizing the receiver.

"Hello. . . . Yes, this is she. . . . Yes. . . . What? . . . That's absurd. I . . . Yes, that's right. . . . No . . . When can we see him? . . . Yes . . . yes." Megan cradled the receiver, turning toward us, but looking at no one in particular.

"What is it, Megan?" Pamsett asked, leaning toward her with a worried expression marring his patrician features.

"Michael," she said woodenly. "He's . . . just confessed . . . to killing Sparky Linville."

SEVEN

The silence lasted perhaps a dozen seconds, but it seemed as if everyone in the room had decided to see how long he could hold his breath. Megan sank into the chair next to the telephone and covered her face with her hands.

"Stop acting so damn dramatic and pull yourself together!" Doyle ordered. "Who was that?"

"A police sergeant," she whispered, letting her fingers slide down her cheeks. "I'm not sure I got his name."

"Stebbins?" I asked.

"That sounds like it. He said Michael had asked him to call us and say he'd made a confession. They must have beat it out of him."

"Wrong," I said emphatically. "This is why I didn't like the sound of things. I knew when I heard he didn't want a lawyer that he must be getting ready to confess."

"But *why?*" Megan was actually plaintive. "Michael is as gentle as a lamb—Lily can tell you that. He couldn't hurt anyone, let alone . . ." She extended her arms, palms up, then let them drop.

"I don't know what your son has said, or admitted to, but you can be sure that if the district attorney's crew knows about Linville's assault of your daughter, they'll hammer on the 'outraged-brother-hell-bent-on-avenging-his-sister' angle, which they can make pretty damning, depending on what other evidence they have. It also means Noreen will be questioned, of course. There is another possibility . . ."

Doyle glared at me. "Don't go coy on us, Goodwin. Let's have it. Unload."

"You hardly need to be a genius like Nero Wolfe to figure it out," I fired back, not liking his tone. "Maybe Michael's decided to sacrifice himself to protect someone."

"Totally ridiculous! Who would he be protecting?" Megan wailed.

"Someone close to him—like maybe a family member." I let my eyes briefly move to Lily, who looked thoughtful.

"That," Megan responded, spacing the words and accenting each one, "is a despicable thing to say. Mr. Goodwin, if you were not such a close friend of my sister's, I would ask you to leave."

"Now, hold on a minute, Megan," Doyle rumbled. "I came in late, but I'm assuming Goodwin is here because he knows something about criminals and murder and how the police operate, that kind of thing."

"He's here because *I* invited him to come with me, and I wouldn't blame him one bit if he got up and walked out that door right now without so much as a backward look." It was Lily, still sitting but tensed, and I could tell she was working to keep her Irish temper from pulling at Mount St. Helens. "But you're right, Doyle; he does know something—a lot *more* than something—about criminals and police and the law, and you'd both damn well better listen to him if you care about what happens to Michael."

Megan continued trying to vaporize me with her eyes, but Doyle nodded his assent to Lily and dropped into a chair. "I hear you," he said. "Okay, Goodwin, the floor is yours—what do you think we ought to do now?"

"The top priority is to get your son a first-rate defense attorney pronto, whether he wants one or not," I said. "I wouldn't trust his case to the public defender's office. It's not that they don't have some talent, but you want a heavy hitter here. I can suggest a few names if you'd like. And I'll also talk to the people at Homicide; I might be able to find out what went on in the interrogation."

"I still can't believe this is happening," Megan whined. "And he wouldn't even phone us himself—he got a damn policeman to do it for him."

"It sounds like he doesn't want to see any of you right now, whatever his reasons," I said gently.

"Well, I'm damned if anyone's going to make me believe Michael's guilty of a thing!" she ranted, pacing again and waving her arms like a hyperactive traffic cop on Fifty-seventh Street. "And you're a lot of help," she hissed at Doyle between puffs of a fresh cigarette. The room was starting to smell like the smoking car on the five-forty-two local to White Plains. "If we waited for you to spring into action, we'd all be in wheelchairs or nursing homes."

"Oh, for God's sake, shut up and stop embarrassing yourself, Megan." Doyle slouched, shaking his head and jamming his hands into his pants pockets.

"Still ready to deliver the witty rejoinder, aren't we? Some things never change—unfortunately," she said with a tight smile. She kept on, but I quit paying attention because I was distracted by the figure that had moved into the doorway at Megan's back.

Although I hadn't seen her for a few years, I immediately recognized the barefoot and bathrobed young woman with the tousled black hair and puzzled blue eyes. Noreen James had matured, in a pleasantly coltish way, since our last meeting. Her face showed a less-pleasant aging, complete with dark circles that ringed those blue eyes, but that very likely was attributable to recent events.

Her father saw her at the same time I did. "Noreen, honey, I didn't know you were here." He got up and moved toward her. "How are you, baby?"

She tensed, drawing back from Doyle, and his face registered something between hurt and puzzlement. "Noreen's been staying here for the last couple of days," Megan said to Lily and me, either ignoring the father-daughter byplay or oblivious of it. "I thought that would be . . . *better*." Her tone implied that no one else was capable of giving the young woman comfort and protection.

"Hello, Nor," Lily said, smiling. "I think you remember Archie Goodwin."

"Oh . . . yes, yes," she said absently, turning to Carmella and asking for coffee. The maid scurried off silently to get another cup. Noreen ran her fingers through her disheveled hair, looking around self-consciously with the realization that she was half-dressed in a room full of fully clothed people, one of whom—me—was a virtual stranger. She thought about it for a few seconds and shrugged, then took two steps toward me, smiled as if we were old friends, and held out a hand, which I took. Now, *that's* aplomb.

Another level of realization was kicking in, though, as she completed the awakening process. She frowned and turned toward her mother. "Why is everyone here?"

Megan got up and went to her, but it was clear from their awkward embrace that mother and daughter were hardly soulmates. "It's because of Michael. He's been . . . well . . ."

"God, stop beating around the bush!" Doyle made a pistol-shot sound by slamming a fist into a palm. "She's an adult, regardless of the way you insist on treating her. Noreen, Michael is being held by the police. From what we know right now, and that's pretty sketchy, your brother has confessed to killing Barton Linville."

That really put Noreen's aplomb to the test, and she came through like Reggie Jackson with runners at second and third and the game on the line. "Michael?

That is totally preposterous," she pronounced firmly, fully awake now and sticking her chin out and shaking her head as she looked from face to face. "Does anybody really believe Michael could do . . . *that*?"

"Of course not, darling," Megan said softly. "And that's what we were talking about when you came in. Mr. Goodwin has been giving us the benefit of his vast knowledge regarding criminal procedures and such." After I set down the preceding sentence, I realized it sounded like Megan was being sarcastic, but that really wasn't the case. The gravity of the situation had fully whacked her, and it seemed apparent that any anger she had felt toward me earlier had been overriden by her concern about her son.

"God, where's a cigarette?" Noreen snapped, her eyes darting around the room.

"Right here." Good old Pamsett, who in an earlier era could have made a dandy living playing Fred Astaire's Man Friday, flicked open a silver case, and after Noreen had selected a cigarette, he put his Dunhill to work with a smooth motion that probably took years to perfect.

Noreen indulged herself in a deep drag, then looked doubtfully at me. "So, you're the expert. I assume you know all about . . . everything. I mean, what happened with Sparky and me. What do you think?" Her aplomb had begun to slip, and her hostility, at least toward me, was rising.

I shot a glance toward Lily, who nodded in the manner of Nero Wolfe, which is to say an eighth-inch dip of the chin. "I know you had a difficult situation a while back," I said evenly.

"You put it very diplomatically," she responded with a tight smile that had no happiness behind it. "What do you think about *Michael's* situation?"

"As I was saying before you came in, your brother is in a grade-A pickle. First off, he apparently has confessed. Second, up to now he has refused legal assistance, which means he'll get a public defender unless someone finds him a lawyer. That's not good. And the way things are looking, he's going to need plenty of horsepower in the courtroom. Third, you'd better believe the D.A. will put a lot of muscle behind this; after all, the son of a big-name, big-money family has been murdered—on the Upper East Side, no less—and the media will be all over him to come up with a quick conviction. And as I was also telling your mother and father, on top of it all, you're sure to be questioned—probably today—about you and Linville."

"I'll handle that when it comes along," Noreen said in a voice just above a whisper, breathing deeply and making her hands into fists. "We're getting a top lawyer, of course?" She directed the question to her father.

"Damn right we are; I'm about to make some calls. Can we get Michael out on bail, Goodwin?"

"Depends on several things, including how forceful your defense attorney is and whether your son has a previous record. Does he?"

"Of course not!" Megan was on her feet again. "I don't think he's ever had anything more than a parking ticket, and hardly any of those. I told you, he's as gentle as a lamb."

"You've made your point, Megan," Lily inserted with quiet force.

I smiled in Lily's direction to show that I appreciated the reinforcements. "Given the circumstances—and assuming you hire a good lawyer—there's a strong chance he'll get out on bond," I told Megan. "But that's only my assessment."

"This is crazy," Noreen said. "I know Michael was furious when he found out what happened to me, but no way would he do something so . . . awful."

"So your mother has stated. But think for a minute about how the whole business looks," I said. "I don't believe it needs to be spelled out for anyone."

"No, no. We've got to do something—I mean

besides hiring some big-deal damned lawyer. Innocent people have gotten convicted before, correct?"

"More than once," I agreed.

"Mr. Goodwin," Noreen implored, sliding in next to me on the sofa and gripping my upper arm so hard it almost hurt, "I want to hire Nero Wolfe. He'll cut through all of this garbage and figure out who really was the murderer, won't he?"

"That's ridiculous!" Megan was glaring first at her daughter and then at me, presumably for putting the notion in Noreen's mind.

"What's ridiculous about it, Mother? Mr. Goodwin, doesn't Nero Wolfe say he's a genius? Don't *you* say he's a genius?" There was a hint of hysteria in Noreen's voice—and her eyes. But there was nothing wrong with her strength, as her hand continued digging into my arm.

"Mr.Wolfe *has* been called a genius on occasion," I conceded. "And there are times when even I am forced to concur, albeit reluctantly."

"Mother, you know Michael isn't a murderer." Noreen released my arm and padded over to Megan. "Daddy knows he isn't, I know he isn't. But if he goes on trial—"

"She's right," Lily put in. "None of us yet has the details of what Michael told the police, but from what little we *do* know, a trial could be a real crapshoot, even if he had Clarence Darrow defending him."

"You're actually suggesting she should hire *Wolfe*?" Megan sounded as appalled as if someone had suggested that Bloomingdale's start selling tractors and cattle feed.

Noreen set her jaw. "Mother, I have the money, if that's what's worrying you. I'm aware that he's expensive."

"Money's the least of our problems right now, Noreen." Megan's voice was sharp enough to slice a diamond. "How do you think it would look if you brought in a private detective who positively wallows in publicity and—"

"I really don't give a damn *how* it would look," Noreen cried. "All I care about is Michael."

I was watching a battle of wills between two women who at least at the moment seemed to be as flexible as an iron reinforcing bar. Once again, Doyle stepped between them. "Honey, that's really all any of us cares about right now," he told Noreen, putting his arm around her. "If you want Wolfe on the case, I'll pay for it."

Noreen yanked away, and her eyes blazed. For an instant I was looking at a younger Lily. "No you won't, Daddy! I'm the reason Michael's in trouble, and I'm going to do something about it. Mr. Goodwin, I want to see Nero Wolfe."

Megan turned away with a theatrical moan of frustration. I'd almost swear Lily was enjoying the show. Under her grim expression, a light danced in her eyes.

"You're assuming a lot," I told Noreen. "Mr. Wolfe works only when he feels like it, and he doesn't feel like it very often. That's part of what makes my job so much fun."

"Then you have to help me persuade him," she said, fixing me with her baby blues. "How soon can we see him? I can be presentable in ten minutes. Let's go."

I gave her a long look with my own baby blues, then glanced at Lily, who smiled mockingly, as if to say: You're the one who claims to know women, pal; don't think you're going to find any help in this corner.

"I'll compromise," I said to Noreen. "I will talk to Mr. Wolfe—alone—about taking you on as a client. I can't guarantee anything; he does what he wants to do, and when he wants to do it. But it works better when I handle him my way. If you don't believe me, ask your aunt; she's known him for years."

Noreen threw a glance at Lily, who backed me up

with a real nod, not one of those eighth-of-an-inch numbers. Noreen's shoulders sagged. "All right," she sighed. "You'll talk to him this morning?"

"As God and Ed Koch are my witnesses," I said, checking my watch. "In fact, I'd better leave now. He will be walking into his office in thirty-seven minutes, and I'd like to be there to greet him."

"And tell him about Michael. And me?" Noreen asked hopefully.

"Noreen, you're making a mistake—a big one," Megan cut in. "You're—"

"For God's sake, leave her alone!" Doyle boomed. "She's capable of making decisions without your damn meddling."

Megan was about to return the salvo when I jumped in. It was that or hang around all day watching the James family bounce rocks off one another's noggins. "When I see an opportune time, I'll talk to Mr. Wolfe," I promised Noreen, ignoring her sparring parents. "As somebody—don't ask me who—once said, 'Timing is everything.' And on this, you'll have to leave the timing to me." As I rose to go, I sent a look in Lily's direction.

"Megan, Doyle, I really must be leaving too," La Rowan said, getting up. "And good-bye, honey," she added with warmth, reaching for Noreen, who buried her face in Lily's shoulder and clung to her a moment.

When we were alone in the southbound elevator, the woman of my life turned to me and rubbed a finger along her graceful chin. "Okay, I caught your not-so-subtle message," she said. "After all, regardless of what you think, I'm not totally dense. What's the problem?"

"Michael," I answered as the elevator disgorged us into the palatial lobby. There was a break in the conversation while the doorman flagged us a cab. "What about him?" Lily said when we were headed south in the taxi of one Luis Ramirez, who had artistically decorated his dashboard with three pairs of pink baby booties.

"I have never met your half-nephew, or whatever the proper terminology is, so I'm flying on instruments," I told her. "And I want your best guess—as in: Did he or didn't he?"

"Kill Linville? Archie, I honestly don't know, but to put it into terms that you're comfortable with, I'd say it's nine-to-five that Michael's innocent. Now, I grant you those odds come courtesy of the suspect's aunt, or half-aunt if you prefer, so you can do your own weighing."

"You like the guy?"

"Michael? Absolutely. He's high-grade. Serious, hardworking—he's in an executive-training program at Metropolitan Trust's headquarters building down on Wall Street."

"Personality?"

Lily's eyes flicked over a display of cocktail dresses in a store window. "Pleasant and engaging, but bordering on the stuffy, which is too bad, although even as a kid he was somewhat that way. But I think that stuffiness has increased since he's been at the bank."

"Not surprising," I observed. The word "kill" had gotten Luis Ramirez's attention. He was leaning at such a slant to get an ear near the opening in the Plexiglas divider that I was a little worried he might topple over. "What's his social life like?"

Lily considered a moment before answering. "He dates a fair amount, but no one special as far as I know. I'm not aware that he runs with a particular crowd—I think it's mostly people he went to school with and from the bank and the financial district. And he's one good-looking guy."

"Again not surprising, especially considering his father."

She gave me an enigmatic look. "Interesting you should say that."

"I didn't realize I was being any more interesting than usual."

"Archie, I feel like I'm exposing you little by little to the foibles—and skeletons—of our family. There's, well, some doubt as to whether Doyle is really Michael's father—at least in Doyle's mind."

"Continue, please." Luis Ramirez was practically quivering with curiosity. We nearly sideswiped a delivery truck.

"Megan apparently had something of a fling ages ago, about the time Michael came along. What little I know about it is from Doyle; we've become pretty close through the years. Needless to say, Megan and I have never discussed the subject."

"I hate to sound like a broken record, but that's hardly surprising. Does Michael know anything about this?"

"Unfortunately, yes, and he blames his mother. And I also know, again from Doyle, that it stimulated more than a little discussion between him and Megan years ago."

"Undoubtedly. But they stayed together for a long time after that?"

"It was one of those marriages that staggered on long after it was dead. The old story—they kept it together mainly for the kids."

"And who is Noreen's father?" I asked.

"Oh, Doyle—I don't have any doubt about it," Lily stated. "By the time she arrived, three years after Michael, Megan's silly liaison had ended. Actually, my impression is that the marriage improved for a few years there."

"I assume the liaison was not with Pamsett."

"Good Lord, no. He's relatively new on the scene. He's a widower, plenty of assets, comes from pharmaceutical money. They met working together on some benefit or other."

"He seems pleasant enough."

Lily shrugged. "I guess so. 'Urbane' and 'cultured' are a couple of good words to describe him, but he's not my type."

"Meaning I'm not urbane and cultured?"

"You, my dear, have more *savoir vivre* than ought to be legal for any one person. And if you don't know what that means, you can always ask your boss."

"I have a pretty good idea." I sniffed, feigning offense, then grinning. "Anything else I ought to know about these intriguing relatives of yours?"

"Heavens, isn't that enough?"

"Yeah, I guess so. I feel like I've wandered into an episode of *Dynasty*. Well, here ye be, lady," I said as the cab pulled up in front of her building. "I'm off to see whether the Living Legend can be persuaded to get involved with the misadventures of the Jameses."

"Good luck. And don't forget to ask him about *savoir vivre*," Lily said as the cab pulled away. I gave her my best smirk in answer, but she was in animated conversation with the doorman and missed it. That's just like her, always getting in the last word.

EIGHT

Mr. Ramirez pulled up in front of the brownstone at ten-fifty-nine, which meant that by the time I'd paid, tipped him, and got Fritz to unbolt the front door, Wolfe already had arranged himself behind his desk and started attacking the morning mail. So much for my being on hand to greet him.

"Good morning, did you sleep well?" I asked with a smile, stealing his own opening line as I sauntered into the office.

Wolfe scowled his opinion of my attempt at humor and then gave me an expression that a six-year-old could have interpreted as: Where the hell have you been?

"Maybe you've been wondering where I've been," I said conversationally as I dropped into my desk chair. "On the other hand, maybe you haven't."

"Archie," he said, allowing himself a protracted sigh that probably reached Fritz's ears in the kitchen, "I could of course feign total uninterest regarding your ambulations, but you would no doubt counter with one of your puerile devices to distract or otherwise bedevil me. The result would be to increase the tension in this environment, which is hardly conducive to proper digestion. Am I correct in stating that your foreday activities centered on Miss Rowan's family?"

"You are."

"All right, confound it, report!" he grumbled, indulging himself in another sigh.

"Yes, sir," I said, making sure to keep my face straight. I then proceeded to give him a verbatim of the events at both Lily's and Megan's apartments. Wolfe listened with eyes closed and fingers laced over his center mound, except when he surfaced to drink beer poured from the first of two bottles Fritz had delivered. He asked no questions, which is out of character, but he made a face several times—which is in character—and managed a full-scale grimace right at the end of my narrative, when I got to the part about Noreen wanting to hire him.

"Bah, refer her to the police. They have the resources to establish her brother's innocence or guilt far more readily than I."

"Hell, the cops already are convinced the brother did it. Besides, that's the easy way out for them—a confession dropped into their laps. No, sir. She wants you. And she says she is willing to pay."

"I am not interested." He reached for his book.

"I can suggest two reasons why you should be," I told him. "One, Lily Rowan; and two, our bank balance. I realize that the latter is in moderately robust health at this moment, but we both know only too well how fast that can change. For one thing, the Mercedes is due for a major tune-up. For another, the heating-and-air-conditioning man is coming next week, and chances are the old furnace is ready for the scrap heap. Remember, you're the one who complained so much last winter about drafts. For yet another, the outside trim has got to be painted and—"

"Archie, shut up!"

"Then there's Lily Rowan, who admires you unabashedly and for whom you also have expressed admiration. This is her niece we're talking about, a young woman ill-used by someone she thought was a friend."

"You have only her word for that," Wolfe remarked, setting his book down deliberately and glaring at me.

"That's true, and now with Linville dead, that's all I'll ever have. But as you have said many times, I am an astute judge of women," I told him, warming to the realization that now I at least had his attention. "And from what little I've seen of Noreen James so far, as well as what Lily has told me, I would be inclined to wager my next paycheck that the young lady had a bad experience, probably a very bad experience, with the late Mr. L."

Wolfe scowled, drained the beer from his glass, and scowled again, opening his center desk drawer and peering in. He was counting bottle caps, a ritual that allows him to monitor his beer consumption. "All right, I will see Miss James. What is her emotional state?" This question is not surprising from a man who has been known to flee from a room at the first hint of tears or other signs of what he perceives—rightly or otherwise—to be female hysteria.

"Unhappy, but plenty stable," I responded. "In many ways, she reminds me of Lily. She has that same blend of warmth, toughness, temper, and brains. And who knows—maybe like her aunt, she will find you charming."

That remark got ignored, as I had expected it would. Wolfe leaned back, eyes closed and hands cupping the arms of his chair. While a visitor might surmise that he was weighing the pros and cons of the prospective case, I knew he was contemplating lunch, because the wonderful aroma of Fritz's spareribs, served with a special sauce he and Wolfe concocted several years back, had begun to permeate the office. I'll confess that I was thinking about lunch myself.

"At the risk of breaking into what might well be a creative reverie, when can you see Noreen?" I asked. "What about this afternoon? Say, three o'clock?"

Wolfe sniffed. " 'Creative reverie' is an oxymoron. I do not indulge in reverie."

But I hadn't spent more than half my life with Wolfe's dictionary for nothing. "Enough with the obfuscation," I told him. "If you don't like three, pick another number. I got the distinct impression Noreen could come at any time convenient to you."

That threw him off, as I had hoped it would. He knows my vocabulary has increased, albeit slowly, through the years, but he's never quite prepared to hear words such as "obfuscation" coming out of my mouth. Maybe he thinks that he's the only one in the brownstone who reads Safire's column in the *Times* Sunday magazine.

"Miss James may come at three," he decreed. "My agreeing to see her, however, does not constitute a contract, and she should be fully cognizant of that."

"I believe she already is well aware of your methods of operation. In fact, I have it on good authority that to ingratiate herself, she is bringing gifts to you, including a new illustrated guide to orchid growing, two cases of Remmers beer, and a collection of London *Times* crossword puzzles. I of course told her that you couldn't be bought by such transparent ploys, but she . . ."

I stopped talking, because I lost my audience. Wolfe had risen and was headed out the office door, his destination being the dining room, where a plate of spareribs awaited him—and me.

NINE

Because any discussion of business is verboten at meals in the brownstone, Noreen James's name didn't come up during lunch. However, as soon as Wolfe and I were back in the office with coffee after having laid waste to the spareribs and the raspberries in sherry cream, I dialed Lily at home.

"Mr. Wolfe can see your niece at three, which is only forty minutes from now," I said. "Can you relay that message to her?"

"I'll be happy to. I owe you something—say, dinner at La Ronde?"

"Sold, although of course I've earned every dollar of that meal. One more thing: As you are well aware, Nero Wolfe's services hardly come cheap. Is your niece, uh . . ."

"My dear chap, if 'loaded' is the word you're groping for, the answer is affirmative, and that's spelled with capital letters. I gather her ability to pay is in question?"

"I wasn't sure if she had an independent source of income, other than her publishing job, that is. Or if she'd have to tap into one of her parents—specifically her mother. I'm not wild about the idea of, in effect, having your half-sister as our client."

"Oh, stop worrying. I don't make it a habit to pry into the financial condition of members of my family, but in Noreen's case, I happen to know—and only because she told me—that on her twenty-first birthday she came into the first payment of a trust fund, and that it brought her something over a million. And there is plenty more on the way a few years down the line in another installment. Unlike my case, it hasn't spoiled her, though; she's worked, by choice, from the day she got out of school, and she is by no means a reckless spender. She does buy nice clothes, though, despite the way she looked this morning. Anyway, the bottom line is that you and Wolfe can charge your usual outrageous fees without having to worry about guilty consciences."

"I never have a guilty conscience," I said, trying to sound offended. "Also, you are not spoiled. Lazy—maybe. Spoiled—never."

"You sweet-talker," she purred. "If you don't hear from me in the next ten minutes, Noreen will be on your doorstep promptly at three."

It was actually seven minutes after three when the doorbell sounded. "That would be Miss James," I said to Wolfe, who gave no sign from behind his book that he had heard me.

Viewed through the one-way panel in our front door, Noreen James looked like a different person from the one I had seen earlier in her mother's apartment. Granted, she had now been awake for several hours, had made up her face and fixed her hair, and was clad in a crisp blue shirtdress with a white belt and white pumps. As Lily said, she does dress well.

"Good afternoon, and please come in," I said with a smile as I swung the door open.

"Hello, again, Mr. Goodwin," she responded primly, returning the smile. "And thank you for getting me such a fast appointment."

"Call me Archie, and thanks aren't necessary. Part of my role is to see that my employer doesn't get rusty from disuse." I ushered Noreen into the office and made the introductions. Lily must have primed her, because she seemed to know that Wolfe is not a hand-shaker.

"I appreciate your seeing me," she said, easing into the red leather chair and keeping her eyes on Wolfe. "I have my checkbook here, and—"

"A moment, Miss James." Wolfe raised a palm. If he was rankled by having a young woman as a prospective client—something that has unsettled him on occasion—he didn't let it show. The man never ceases to amaze me. "My agreeing to talk to you does not necessarily signify a contract between us. That may result, but not until I know considerably more than is now the case."

"All right," Noreen said, folding her hands in her lap and meeting his eyes squarely. She seemed undaunted by Wolfe and his size, which endeared her to me. "But first, I have to tell you both the news: Michael is out on bond. My father took your advice, Mr. Goodwin—Archie. His attorney recommended a criminal lawyer, his name is Hargrove, and this man argued that Michael has no record and that his family is well-known. So now he's free."

"At least for the moment," I remarked. "But, hey, that's a victory of sorts. And from what little I know about Hargrove, you've got yourself a top-flight man."

Wolfe snorted, which was meant to reflect his opinion of lawyers in general. "Before we begin, Miss James, may I offer you something to drink? I'm having beer, but Mr. Goodwin can get you any one of a variety of beverages." She said no thanks and Wolfe rang for beer, readjusting his bulk.

"Very well. Mr. Goodwin has supplied me with some basic information, but I have myriad questions, a few of a personal nature."

"I'm ready."

"First, how did you meet Mr. Linville?"

"Through my roommate—Polly Mars. She and I went to college together, at Smith, and for the last two years we've shared an apartment on the Upper West Side. She's a fashion model, kind of struggling at it, but getting herself a few jobs."

"And where did Miss Mars make the acquaintance of Mr. Linville?"

"At Orion—that's a bar up on Second Avenue where a lot of people our age hang out."

"You among them?"

She colored slightly. "Oh, I've *been* there a couple of times with Polly," she said, brushing her hair back from her forehead. "But I'm not really into those places. They're awfully noisy for one thing, and most of the people are phonies, if you know what I mean."

Wolfe didn't know, and didn't care. "So Miss Mars brought you together?"

"Not directly," Noreen said, crossing one slim leg over the other and smoothing her skirt. "Actually, she had several dates with . . . Sparky, and the first time I met him was when they came back to our apartment one night after hitting a few of the places. I could tell he was interested in me, and a couple days later he called and asked me to go out."

"How did Miss Mars react to this?"

"That was the first thing that occurred to me, as you might imagine," Noreen said. "She knew before she ever went out with him that he had a reputation for being pretty wild, but from what I could tell, and from our talks, she was having a good time with him. Anyway, when he called me and asked me out, I didn't say yes right away; I put him off, asked him to call back later. And then I told Polly about it. She said it didn't bother her at all, that she was getting tired of going to the same places with him—like Orion and Morgana's. You should see Polly, Mr. Wolfe. She's really beautiful, tall and blond. She's never had trouble getting dates. She's gone out with guys just as rich and well-known as Sparky, so being around him was no big deal with her."

"Did she warn you about anything?" Wolfe asked.

"You mean . . ." She took a deep breath, then shook her head vigorously. "No. And I got the impression nothing much went on between them. But I didn't ask her during the time they were seeing each other, and she didn't volunteer any details. We're pretty good friends, but we don't talk about . . . *that* with each other, never have."

I knew Wolfe was uncomfortable with the subject. But I also was aware, given his respect and admiration for Lily, that he was willing to tough it out, at least for a while.

"So you agreed to an engagement with Mr. Linville?"

"Yes, and we had a very good time that first night. To be honest, I was a little worried beforehand. Most of the guys I've gone out with, at least until recently, have been, you know, fairly conservative. Maybe that's because I'm what you'd call conservative too, I guess. And I'd have to say I was flattered by the attention. Anyway, on our first date we went to a comedy revue down in the Village, which was very funny. Then we had a couple of drinks at Morgana's, where we ran into some of his friends, and then he took me home—all very innocent. God, was I fooled. Talk about a babe in the woods."

Wolfe drank beer and glowered at his nearly empty glass. "So there was a second engagement?"

Noreen nodded. "Right. By now, I was thinking Sparky Linville was just an exuberant rich young guy whose activities had gotten blown out of proportion by the papers. And there was even something about him in *People* or *Us* one time, I think. Anyway, yes, I did go out with him again—once."

Wolfe contemplated her but said nothing. She returned the look, then glanced my way. Only a stone-heart could fail to have sympathy for her at this point, and even Wolfe isn't a stone-heart. We both waited for her to continue.

"So the second time we went out, on a Saturday night, it was just for drinks, to—where else?—Orion and then Morgana's. He took me home early and invited himself up. Polly was gone for the weekend, staying with her folks up in Bronxville."

"Did Mr. Linville know your roommate was away?" Wolfe asked.

"Not that I'm aware of, although I guess I must have mentioned it when we got upstairs. Anyway, we each had a beer, I turned on some music, and . . ." She braced her shoulders. Wolfe leaned back, closing his eyes, then took a breath, came forward in his chair, and started to say something, but Noreen cut him off.

"Before you ask the question, I'll answer it for you, Mr. Wolfe," she said, measuring her words. "I did not—repeat, *did not*—do anything to lead him on or encourage him. I've thought about it at least a dozen times every day since it happened, and I know I did absolutely nothing to make him think I was . . ." Her voice was a little wobbly.

"I was not about to pose that question, Miss James," Wolfe responded evenly. "What I was about to ask was if you saw or spoke to Mr. Linville after that night."

Noreen's voice strengthened. That was good. Wolfe probably was shaking in his brown wing-tips, worried she might burst into tears.

"I didn't see him again—not ever. He phoned three or four times, and I hung up when I heard his voice. He called Polly at least twice and asked her to get me to the phone, but when she told me who it was, I wouldn't talk to him."

"Did you tell Miss Mars what had transpired?"

"No, but she pretty much figured it out from the way I guess I was acting, plus the fact that I had a small bruise on one cheek, although I told her that was from falling on a bus when the driver slammed on the brakes. She kept asking what had happened between Sparky and me. I wouldn't tell her—I just couldn't. I couldn't tell anybody." Noreen took a couple of deep breaths, but gave a negative wave of the hand when I asked if she wanted a drink. All the color was gone from her face.

"Whom did you tell—and when?" Wolfe asked. I was probably the only person alive who could detect that he was moved by the narrative.

"Aunt Lily was really the first, and that was just this last Saturday, when we had brunch," she said. "I'd been carrying it around with me for weeks. My mother was away, or she surely would have figured something out, and Michael and I hadn't been together lately—no particular reason, just our separate lives. Same with Daddy, I hadn't seen much of him for a couple of months. And actually, I didn't even tell Aunt Lily *who* did it, just that it was someone I'd gone out with. She figured it out, though. She knew I'd been out with Sparky. And I think she said she'd been introduced to him, I forget exactly where."

"So Mr. Linville knew Miss Rowan?"

"Uh . . . yes—at least they'd met," Noreen said. "Why?"

"And was he also aware that Miss Rowan and Mr. Goodwin are good friends?" Wolfe asked, ignoring her question.

Noreen wrinkled her face. "Mm, it might have come up. I vaguely remember mentioning something to him after Aunt Lily's name had come up in conversation, what with Mr. Goodwin being so . . . well-known and all."

Wolfe allowed himself a slight grimace at the mention of my renown. "When did your mother learn what had transpired with Mr. Linville?"

"She got home Tuesday from Europe, and Michael and I had an informal little welcome-back party—at her place. You know, champagne, a few balloons, a sign on the door. We invited Edward—Mr. Pamsett—too, because he and Mother have been what you might call an item for some time now, a few years, I guess. I worked extra hard to look good and act cheerful. But Mother saw right through me."

"And she managed to worm it out of you?"

"I'll say. I guess I sort of went to pieces. Some celebration *that* turned out to be! I really put a damper on the big homecoming." She looked down, pleating the skirt of her dress with her fingers.

"So on Tuesday night, not only your mother but also your brother and Mr. Pamsett knew what had happened," Wolfe asked rhetorically. "I assume they also learned that the other party was Mr. Linville?"

Noreen nodded. "Mother was almost hysterical, which I suppose you can attribute partly to the jet lag, but through all her rantings she seemed mainly freaked-out that the newspapers would get hold of the story. Heaven help us if the sainted family name gets sullied, you know? And *now* what's likely to happen to the family name in the media? Michael went nuts. I've never seen him so mad. In fact, he hit a glass-topped cocktail table so hard with his fist that he put a crack in it. Edward stayed his usual laid-back self, though. He thought we ought to go to the police, which really made Mother crazy."

"Can you recall what your brother said?"

"Oh, he was furious. He started yelling about how I should have been happy to be going out with Doug. But he was only mad at himself. You know, for not being able to protect me."

"Doug?"

"That's somebody I see fairly often, Douglas Rojek. And then he began yelling about how people like . . ." Noreen took a deep breath, then another, as if she couldn't bear to pronounce the name. ". . . like *him* are treated in other countries when they get caught doing . . . well, you know. He was pretty . . . graphic."

"Did he make any specific threats at that time involving Mr. Linville?"

"No, just rantings. But that's Michael—he's mostly bark. I've never known him to even throw a punch at anyone, except as a college boxer, and he only did that to fulfill his sports requirement. Violence is not in his nature."

"So noted," Wolfe remarked dryly. "But let us for a moment consider this consecution: A young woman is outrageously ill-used by a flamboyant and wealthy libertine. Soon thereafter, this debauchee is found dead, an apparent murder victim. The young woman's protective and outraged older brother, apprehended by the police, although not resisting them, readily confesses to the slaying. You must admit we have here, especially from the law-enforcement perspective, a compelling scenario. Were I a district attorney, I would relish such a situation."

Noreen bristled. "You sound like an enemy rather than a friend."

Wolfe regarded her beatifically. "It is most often friends who tell us what we least wish to hear."

She looked at him doubtfully, then turned to me for a reaction. I raised one eyebrow and smiled.

"Oh, you're right, of course," she said, shifting nervously in the red leather chair. "I'm sorry for flaring up, but I'm positive Michael is innocent. Won't you please help?"

Wolfe considered her and then looked at the wall clock, confirming that his afternoon sojourn with the orchids was perilously close at hand. "Madam," he said, "you no doubt are aware that my fees are what some have termed exorbitant."

"I am aware of that. I can afford you."

He closed his eyes and coupled his hands over his center mound. I knew he was trying to figure out a good reason why he should turn Noreen down. Work was bad enough; a woman client was worse. But he also knew that if he gave her a thumbs-down, he'd have to listen to me carping about the bank balance. Simply put, the big guy was between the proverbial rock and hard place. After thirty seconds he opened his eyes and considered Noreen without enthusiasm.

"Very well. I accept your commission, but with

two provisos: First, I cannot, and will not, guarantee success, if you define success as the exoneration of your brother. I will of course explore avenues that seem most likely to bring forth another candidate as Mr. Linville's murderer. Second, I will likely need to speak to some of your acquaintances—among them Miss Mars and perhaps the gentleman of whom you spoke that you see with some regularity. Mr. . . . ?"

"Rojek. Doug Rojek."

"Yes. In the course of my and Mr. Goodwin's conversations with them and with others, it is probable that your unfortunate experience with Mr. Linville will be unavoidably brought into the discussion. Is this of overriding concern to you?"

Noreen blinked twice. "Just yesterday, I would have said yes, but now, what happened to me doesn't seem very important anymore. My brother is innocent, Mr. Wolfe. Ask anybody anything that you think will help Michael."

"That is a pragmatic position to take, Miss James," Wolfe said. For him, the tone was almost approving. "And now I must leave for a previous engagement. However, Mr. Goodwin will work with you on details and specifics." Having thus spoken, Wolfe levered himself to his feet and made for the hall and the elevator.

What Wolfe means by "details and specifics" is, among other things, the discussion of our fees with the client. And since he doesn't like to trouble himself with the specifics of such mundane and mercenary considerations, he leaves them to me—knowing full well that as chief bookkeeper, checkbook-balancer, and bill-payer, I will always make sure that our income is sufficient to cover niceties including the fresh fish, meat, and vegetables that Fritz insists on ordering; the cases of beer that Wolfe insists on consuming; and the salaries that Theodore, Fritz, and I insist on receiving. So far, we always have had enough Federal Reserve notes coming in to ensure that life in the brownstone will continue to function in the manner to which Wolfe long ago became accustomed. For that, I take more than a little of the credit.

"Now, Miss James," I said, swiveling to face our guest after Wolfe had departed for the plant rooms, "before we go any further, let's talk about details and specifics."

TEN

So now we officially had a client, and one who didn't seem to show the slightest resentment about our "outrageous fees." In fact, when I quoted the amount—sixty thousand dollars, half payable now, half at the completion of our work—she simply said, "Oh, I thought it probably would be more." Then, without missing a beat, she pulled out a checkbook with a red-and-blue-plaid cover and proceeded calmly to write out a draft for thirty grand as if it were something she did every time she bought groceries. And she followed by asking me what was next.

"Next is more questions, if you've got the time," I told her with a smile.

"Of course I've got the time, Mr. Goodwin—oh, there I go again. Archie, I mean. Take as long as you want. If anything, I should be concerned about *your* time," Noreen said earnestly, sitting erect in the red leather chair like a student about to be quizzed by a teacher. I could see why Lily was so fond of her; this one had at least two of the three traits I like most—character and manners. The third is a sense of humor, and given the situation, Noreen hadn't had much call to exhibit that side of her, assuming it existed.

I started in with the questions, including how well she felt she'd gotten to know Linville on their two dates.

"Apparently not very well at all, given what happened," she mused. "As I told you and Mr. Wolfe, I really felt that he was an innocent kind of wild, if that makes sense. Not the mean kind, you know? I decided the press must have been unfair about him."

"What about his drinking?"

"Well, he did do a little too much of that for my taste, especially given that he mixed it with driving. I guess if I'd known him better, or longer, I would have eventually said something about it."

"Did you meet any of his friends?"

"Two or three. There was one, Todd Halliburton, we ran into both times we went out."

I remembered Linville's fireplug-sized sidekick. "What was he like?"

Noreen shrugged. "Okay, I guess. Actually, pretty nice. Seemed sort of on the shy side, though. He didn't say much."

I wondered if we'd met the same Halliburton. "Was he with a date? And what did he look like?"

"No, once he was alone—that was at Orion—and the other time, at Morgana's, I think . . . um, yes, it was at Morgana's, he was with another guy, Charlie something, I forget the last name. What did Todd look like? Well, he's really short—shorter than Sparky . . . was. He's got real light hair, almost white, and he wears it cut short. Why?"

"Just curious," I told her. We were talking about the same guy, all right. "What does Halliburton do?"

She frowned, thinking about it. "I think he's an accountant of some kind downtown. He mentioned it one night, but I can't recall. I *do* remember that he said he lived in the Village, but that's about all."

"Miss James, to your knowledge, before Wednesday night who was aware of what had happened between you and Sparky Linville?"

"I thought we were going to use first names," she said with a tight smile. "It's Noreen, remember—*Archie?* Well, as I said before, Lily knew, back last Saturday, and Mother, Michael, and Edward found out when we had that homecoming party. And Daddy knew that same night, of course, because Mother phoned him."

"Do the two of them communicate a lot?"

"I wouldn't say a lot, no. They're not chummy by any means, but they do still talk, especially when it involves Michael or me. And Mother did give Daddy a call that night, to tell him about it. She really hit the ceiling."

"Not so surprising for a mother to be distraught in that situation, though, is it?"

"No," Noreen conceded, "it's not. And I guess I'd have reacted the same way if it had been my daughter."

"Tell me about your friend Rojek, the one you said you see fairly often."

She ran a hand through her hair and let it drop into her lap. "Doug's a nice guy—really sweet. I met him through Michael. They got to know each other in a Wall Street softball league—they were each captain of a company team. Doug's with a brokerage house— Maxwell and Mills."

"Is this serious between you two?"

Noreen's cheeks got rosy again. "I'm not really sure yet, but . . . maybe. I guess it's really a little too early to tell."

"How does he feel about you?"

She paused to think about it. "Well, I have to say I think he's pretty interested, although like me, he's been going out with other people too, at least occasionally."

"Does Rojek know about what happened with Sparky Linville?"

"This may sound funny, but I'm not really sure."

"It does sound funny. After you explain it, maybe I'll understand."

She looked over at the bookcases and then at the globe before answering. "Doug and I have been going out, oh, about once a week for a few months now—to the movies, for drinks, to a Mets game once. As I said, he's really sweet, a nice guy. Well, after what happened with Sparky, I got so depressed, you know, that I didn't feel like seeing Doug—or anybody, for that matter. So I turned him down three or four times in a row. I gave different excuses, like I wasn't feeling well, or I had to spend the evening with Daddy, or I was just plain 'busy,' or—"

"I've been on the receiving end of all of those too, at one time or another," I said, nodding.

She smiled weakly. "Anyway, I knew Doug was getting a little bent out of shape by all the turndowns, so I started saying yes again and we went out a few times, but I knew he could tell something was wrong. I mean, as hard as I tried, I wasn't myself. I'm really still not . . . at all." She allowed herself a deep breath.

"Okay, so he figured out that for some reason you were acting differently. But did he even know you'd gone out with Linville?"

"I'm not sure, unless Polly said something to him."

"Why would she say anything?" I asked. "Was she really miffed after all about you going out with someone she'd been dating?"

"No, I don't think so, I really don't. But Polly seemed to feel Doug was the right person for me, and she was always real friendly to him when he came by to pick me up or when he stopped over for a beer. She always built him up to me when we were alone, and I also think—although I don't know this for sure—that he would call Polly to, you know, talk about me."

"Ah, it's the old story," I said, waving a hand. "Lovestruck lad seeks advice from the best girlfriend of the object of his affection."

"Something like that," Noreen replied, this time favoring me with a sheepish but full-blown smile.

"All right, so it seems likely that Mr. Rojek knew you had been out with Barton Linville. But as to whether he knows anything about *that* night, and what happened, you're not sure at all?"

"No. He never has mentioned Sparky's name, not once. But then, Doug wouldn't. If he's the jealous type, he's never shown it to me. Wait a minute Mr. —Archie," she said, looking directly at me. "Do you think that Doug would have . . . ?" She let the sentence evaporate.

"Right now I don't think anything," I said evenly. "Understand, at this point we are operating on the assumption that your brother had nothing to do with the violent death of one Barton Linville. That being the case, someone else conked Mr. L. in that parking garage. Now, it's possible that Linville had dozens of people you've never met or heard of lining up to give him a one-way trip, but not very likely. The circles he appears to have moved in favor hot air and bluster and posturing—that type wouldn't be apt to resort to murder. Chances are stronger that the person who dispatched him is someone you know—and care for. I mention that because even if your brother is cleared, you may not like the way this business turns out."

"I know," she said softly, shaking her head and looking at the tips of her shoes.

"I honestly don't know how you were able to bottle this up for a whole month," I told her. "Didn't you at least see a doctor?"

"Yeah, I did. And that . . . was really hard." Noreen chewed her lower lip and allowed as to how she could use a glass of water, which I got from the chilled carafe on the table that doubles as a service bar. She thanked me and took a couple of healthy swallows. "He's somebody a friend of mine goes to—no way was I about to call the doctor my mother and I use. Anyway, I made up a story about . . . getting carried away one night, and he gave me a whole batch of tests for, you know . . . everything. God, it was awful."

"Sorry to be so damned nosy, but it's an occupational necessity. Next rough question: Weren't you afraid Linville might . . . be back?"

"Umm, in a way, but for one thing, I, well, sort of *hurt* him, you know?"

"You mean physically?"

Noreen nodded, finishing the rest of her water.

"Dare I ask how?"

"Oh, not what you're probably thinking," she said, coloring slightly. "I scratched him pretty good on the face, for one thing. And I hit him in the eye—I know that hurt because he . . . yelled. Loud. I shouldn't say this, but . . . I wish I'd killed him." She sounded like she meant it.

"Did you kill him, Noreen?" I said, keeping my expression impassive.

She held my eyes for several seconds without blinking, then scraped at a tooth with her thumbnail. "No, but I've had a lot of dreams the last few weeks—nightmares, really—where I, well, murdered him different ways," she said with a quavering voice. "I know that sounds terrible, but I keep getting them—the nightmares, I mean."

I studied her, trying to factor out the histrionics, then decided there weren't any. Whatever neighborhood in my brain decides such things told me I was getting it straight, without any malarkey.

Noreen seemed to sense that I was processing what she'd said, and she waited a discreet period before speaking. "You're really convinced that he was killed because of what happened to me, aren't you?"

"Given the timing, it looks that way. You'd kept quiet about the episode for more than a month, and it didn't come out until a few days ago. And then, not much more than twenty-four hours later, Linville is dead. You have any other theories?"

Her lower lip was getting a workout. "None, but it *is* possible, isn't it, that this could have been something else? Like a robbery—you know, someone hiding in a parking garage waiting for a person who drives an expensive car to pull in late at night, when nobody is likely to be around?"

"In this city, anything's possible," I admitted. "But chances are somebody trying a holdup would have a gun or would make you think they had a gun—as intimidation, not with any intent to use it. But somebody carrying a sap is ready for action."

"A sap?"

"Blackjack, truncheon, tire iron, wrench, whatever. Last I knew, the police hadn't found the weapon."

"But one thing's sure—it must have been a man who did it, right?" she asked.

"I'm sorry to be so indefinite about everything, but even that isn't a sure thing. I know of cases where women have wielded some pretty mean shillelaghs. For openers, Mr. Wolfe once helped send a female from Bayside to prison for life because of the way she'd used a baseball bat on her husband. Anybody with any strength at all can unload at least a stunning blow with, say, a wrench, especially if the target doesn't expect it. And after the first whack, the rest is—"

"Please, don't go on!" Noreen cried, covering her ears. "It's . . . awful."

"Violent death *is* awful. It's only on TV shows that it gets sanitized. End of sermon."

She nodded woodenly. "All right, I think you've laid things out pretty clearly for me. What happens next?"

"Next Mr. Wolfe and I confer and I get instructions. But you already know something about our plans from what Mr. Wolfe said: I'll want to see your brother, your roommate, your friend Rojek. I'll also probably be asking to talk to both your mother and father again. And that's just for starters."

"How long will all this take?"

"That's hard to say, but I'll tell you one thing: It's tough to get Nero Wolfe into high gear. I can push him better than anyone else on the planet, but even then, it's like trying to get a charcoal fire going without starter fluid. All I can promise is that I'll do my best. But before you go, one more question."

"Yes?"

"What were you doing Wednesday night after nine o'clock?"

"I was at my mother's. Why? Oh!" she said, jerking upright. "I know why. Because you want to know where I was when . . . *he* was killed."

"That's right, client or not. Mr. Wolfe will have expected me to ask."

Her cheeks blazed the color of my favorite power tie and she reached into her purse for a cigarette, which she lit with a match before I could produce a lighter. Whatever anger she felt about the question she was working hard to suppress.

"Well, the truth is, I *was* out part of the evening. I was so depressed about Tuesday night, you know, with Mother and everything, that I went out walking for, oh, several hours. Just to get out of the house and away from everybody."

"I suppose you were alone?"

She nodded. "I went east, over around Beekman Place and Sutton Place, and also walked up and down First and Second avenues."

"About what time was this?"

"I was gone from maybe nine-forty-five to twelve-thirty or so. To be honest, I didn't look at my watch once while I was walking."

"And you didn't see anyone you know the whole time?"

She shook her head. "Nobody I knew. The streets were crowded, especially Second Avenue, but, no. Does all this make *me* a suspect?" she snapped.

"Not necessarily, but it could come up at some point. Anyway, I think I've covered everything I need to know for now. I'll keep you apprised of our progress when there are developments, but in the meantime, feel free to call me. Fair enough?"

"Fair enough." She stood and held out a hand. She wasn't smiling, but that's okay; I prefer people whose faces accurately reflect their feelings and, as I suggested earlier, Noreen James didn't have a great deal to smile about at the moment.

ELEVEN

I spent what was left of Friday, not counting dinner, trying to get Wolfe to discuss the James-Linville case, but he wasn't having any, and when he digs his heels in, there's not a lot I can do, despite my bragging to Noreen that I am able to push him better than anybody else on the globe.

I finally gave up after we'd been in the office for about an hour following dinner. "Lord knows, I don't ask a lot," I had said to the covers of the open book that hid Wolfe's face from me. "Just a set of basic instructions to get me moving in the right direction. Here we've taken money from this trusting young woman, who for whatever reasons has confidence in your detecting abilities. At this very moment she probably is sitting at home wondering about how you are progressing on this—"

Wolfe set his book down deliberately and fixed me with a glare that would have done credit to Bela Lugosi. "Archie, you are becoming a Momus."

"Yes, sir. I must be getting edgy because of that maddening middle-class Midwestern conscience of mine; you know, the one that whispers to me that I should be industrious at all times." That sentence and a few more variations on the same theme accomplished absolutely nothing, other than to send Wolfe back to the sanctuary of his book. I sulked at my desk for several minutes, then got up, yawned loudly, and walked out.

It wasn't as though I had nothing to do: Just before dinner, Saul Panzer had called to announce that he was putting together an impromptu poker game that night. Normally, a group of us gets together at Saul's on Thursdays, but this was a bonus session, called by the host because an old friend was passing through town. "You don't give a guy much notice, do you?" I had told Saul at the time, saying the odds were against my making it because we were working on a case. Now, however, with Wolfe having gone into hibernation, I was only too glad to get out of the house, which I did.

I'd like to report that the evening spent with spades, hearts, diamonds, clubs, chips, and five other dollar-ante gamblers was a success, but in truth I was forced to open my wallet several times during the evening to underwrite my continued participation, and when a merciful halt was called to the hostilities a little before one, I was able to say that I had added to the financial well-being of at least three of my tablemates.

So much for Friday. The next morning, I was determined to somehow jump-start Wolfe. The Saturday routine in the brownstone is exactly like that on weekdays, with the lord and master of the manor devoting his standard four hours—two in the morning and two before dinner—to his orchids. So I knew I wouldn't have a crack at him until he came down from the plant rooms at eleven, being as how he views interruptions during his playtime about the same way he views anyone who dares to use "contact" as a verb in his presence.

Both morning papers had stories on young Michael James's arrest, with the *Daily News* splashing it on page one in the form of a photo showing Michael with his lawyer just after he made bond. His head was down in the picture, which was headlined ARREST IN YUPPIE MURDER, and the lawyer was putting up an arm, presumably to shield his client—but not himself—from the glare of publicity. Even the *Times* gave the story front-page play, with a two-column headline in the lower-right-hand corner and a short, relatively unenlightening story about Michael's arrest and release along with biographical information on both Megan and Doyle James that stressed their well-upholstered life-styles. But both stories reported that Michael had given no motive as to why he killed Linville.

I knew Wolfe had digested all of this too, because he reads two papers thoroughly while demolishing the breakfast Fritz delivers on a tray to his bedroom.

After my own breakfast, I busied myself typing letters and massaging the orchid-germination records in the personal computer. I'd run out of work by ten-twenty and was trying to improve my vocabulary by working the *Times* crossword puzzle when the intercom line on the phone rang, meaning I was getting a rare call from Wolfe during his orchid session.

"I have instructions," he said, his tone clearly indicating his displeasure at conducting business from the plant rooms.

"Shoot."

"I believe Mr. Linville's funeral is later today. You should be present."

"It's at twelve-thirty, and I'd been planning to go—whether or not you asked."

He grunted and went on. "I also would like to see Inspector Cramer at eleven."

"This morning?"

"Of course," he answered testily. Wolfe always assumes the entire world is poised for an invitation to the brownstone.

"And if he can't make it then?"

"He'll make it. Tell him Michael James is our client. And ask Miss Rowan to be here this afternoon at three. You should be back by then. Further, I wish to see Michael James tonight. Nine o'clock. His sister may wish to accompany him. However, if she does, I will insist on conversing with Mr. James alone."

"All right. What else?"

"The what-else is yet to be determined, but it is probable that you will have assignments for tomorrow."

"On Sunday? My day off? I've got box seats for the Mets-Cardinals game."

"Give them away," Wolfe sniffed. He had me and he knew it. I was mad because of the likelihood of missing the game but at the same time pleased because he appeared to be using his mental faculties. I went to work, starting with Lily, who was at home.

"Mr. Wolfe would like the pleasure of your company," I purred into the mouthpiece. "This afternoon, no less. At three."

"We're flattered," she responded with a purr of her own, better than mine. "May I assume this has something to do with Michael, or has your boss finally succumbed to my not inconsiderable charms?"

"Some of each, no doubt, although he's requesting your pleasure ostensibly because of the former."

"See you at three, then, lover. Ta-ta."

"Ta-ta, yourself," I said, hanging up and dialing Cramer. I got a sergeant whose name I didn't recognize who said the inspector wasn't available. I told him Nero Wolfe was calling, and that it was important. A pause followed, then muffled conversations.

"Wolfe?" It was Cramer, who didn't sound like he'd just won the lottery. "What is it?"

"It's Goodwin, calling for Mr. Wolfe," I said. "He wondered if you could stop by, say at eleven?"

"Why the hell should I? Is he announcing that he's moving to Montenegro?"

"Nothing so exciting. He's taken on Michael James as a client, and I suppose he wants to talk about the case."

Cramer spat a word but apparently wasn't happy with the pronunciation because he spat it again. "I knew it. The minute I learned you were involved in all this—ah, hell." He slammed his receiver down, which I took to be an acceptance of our invitation.

I then dialed Megan James's apartment, where

Noreen had said she would be staying for the weekend. Carmella answered and after asking who I was called our real client to the phone. "Archie! Has anything happened?" Noreen asked in an out-of-breath tone.

"Nothing you don't know about," I told her. "How's Michael?"

"He's . . . 'distant' I guess is the best way to put it," she said. "He hasn't wanted to talk to anyone since he got, you know . . . out."

"Is he staying there?"

"Yes, for now. He's pretty much closed himself in one of the bedrooms. The lawyer we have, Mr. Hargrove, said he shouldn't go back to his apartment while he's out on bond. He doesn't want him accessible to the press or anyone else. He doesn't want him talking to anybody."

"Well, something's got to give, then, because Mr. Wolfe needs to see Michael—tonight."

"I'm not sure I can get him there, not the way he's been acting." Noreen sounded worried.

"Try hard. You've hired Mr. Wolfe, and even though he's a genius, at least some of the time, he can't do a hell of a lot without talking face-to-face with the accused."

There was a silence before she answered. "All right, I'll do everything I can. What time should I tell him?"

"Nine."

"Should I come too?"

"Not necessary. If playing chaperon is the only way you can get him here, okay, but Mr. Wolfe probably will ask you to wait in the front room while they talk."

I phoned upstairs to Wolfe, filling him in on my calls and getting a grumble for my trouble. Five minutes later, I heard the whirr of the elevator, marking his descent from his posy paradise.

"You're early," I said when he got settled in his chair and began attacking the mail.

"Early? Perhaps by one minute," he said, raising his eyebrows. "I had completed a delicate repotting—there was nothing more to accomplish this morning." Heaven forbid he would ever admit to altering his schedule, even slightly, for a visit from anyone, let alone an officer of the law. As it turned out, he hadn't needed to come down early, and when he finished the small and uninteresting stack of mail, he plunged into his book.

At five past eleven when the doorbell rang, I let Fritz do the honors; Cramer was riled enough without having to deal with me as an official greeter again. It didn't seem to matter who opened the door to him, though, because he barreled into the office like a locomotive under full throttle anyway.

"All right, dammit," he bellowed, jabbing a thick forefinger at Wolfe as he steamed toward the red leather chair, "you've got my attention. What is all this crap about you and Michael James?"

"I assume Mr. Goodwin was lucid during your telephone dialogue," Wolfe responded mildly, closing his book and marking the place with the gold strip he was given by an appreciative client years ago.

"For God's sake, the kid has confessed!" Cramer roared. "He says—or rather, he said once—that he bumped off Linville. Now, of course, his Harvard lawyer is squawking that the confession came under duress."

"Did it?"

Cramer used his favorite word again, this time only once. "Hah, he practically handed it to us when he came down to headquarters."

"Which raises a point," Wolfe said. "What led you to Mr. James in the first place?"

"What difference does that make?" the inspector retorted, coming forward in the chair.

"Quite possibly it is of no significance whatever,"

Wolfe conceded. "But the question seems innocent enough."

Cramer squirmed and pulled a cigar from his breast pocket, jamming it into his mouth. "I had men out asking questions in the bars Linville was known to frequent. One of them talked to a bartender at that Orion place who said Michael James was there looking for Linville the night he was killed, and that he, James, was hot—really hot. Said he wanted to find Linville because of—" Cramer snapped his mouth shut and narrowed his eyes, looking at me, then back at Wolfe and at me again.

"Go on," Wolfe prodded.

"I assume both of you know why James was looking for Linville. Oh, hell, of course you do, what with Goodwin here being such a good friend of Lily's." Cramer scowled. "And that also explains why Goodwin was mixing it up with Linville out in front of Morgana's, right? But I still want to hear *you* say why young James was so fired up that night," he went on, pointing his cigar at Wolfe. "I need to know that you know."

"Of course you do," Wolfe said, inclining toward Cramer and spreading his hands palms down on the desk blotter. "As indeed you should, before you tell us any more. This is a sensitive matter. To put your mind at ease, Archie and I are aware of what apparently transpired between Mr. Linville and Miss James—the occurrence that aroused Michael James's anger."

Cramer snorted. "All right," he said in a tired voice, shaking his head slowly. "This has taken a lot out of me, dammit. You're aware that I've known the family for most of my life. Hell, I knew their father before Lily and Megan were born—Rowan helped get me on the force. You know that. I feel damn near related to those kids." He looked at Wolfe and set his jaw. "Not that it would ever interfere with my job," he said, daring contradiction.

"How did the bartender know Michael James's identity?"

"He'd spent some evenings in that Orion spot himself," Cramer said. "I'm told it's quite a meeting place for the yuppies and preppies and whatever."

Wolfe winced at the terms. "And young Mr. James told the bartender why he wanted to see Barton Linville?"

"In effect. Apparently he stormed in with a snootful and did some hollering about Linville, wanting to know if he'd been around that evening and saying he had a score to settle with him. Noreen's name apparently got mentioned once or twice. The bartender said the way Mike talked, it didn't take an Einstein to figure out what must have happened between Linville and Noreen."

"And what happened when you took Mr. Linville in for questioning?"

"Like I said before, he practically spilled it all when he walked in the door. Said he'd looked for Linville in a few of his haunts—Morgana's, Orion, a couple of other joints—then went by his apartment and tried to get in. The doorman on duty confirmed that for us and identified Mike as having been there that night around twelve-thirty, drunk as a skunk and demanding to see Linville, who of course wasn't home. Then, Mike says, he started walking west on Seventy-seventh, when who should pull into the parking garage a few doors down in his brand new Porsche but Linville.

"Mike says he followed the Porsche into the garage on foot, while the big doors were still open. He says that just inside the doors he found a tire iron and went over to the Porsche, which Linville had by this time parked. He was getting out of the car when Mike called him a bastard, telling him he knew what happened between him and Noreen. Linville took a swing and James coshed him with the tire iron—not once, but several times, he said. Claimed he couldn't stop himself, didn't want to stop himself."

"Did Michael James ever tell you why he wanted to kill Linville?" Wolfe asked.

"Nope," Cramer said, folding his arms. "Some notion of protecting his sister's honor and reputation, I guess. Every time we asked him about it, he clammed up. Wouldn't discuss Noreen at all."

"Have you found the weapon?"

"Not yet. Mike says he ran out of the garage and can't remember what he did with the iron. Apparently he wasn't seen—there's nobody on duty that time of night, and permit parkers, which is all they allow, have to open the auto door with a key."

"And you believe that story?"

Cramer made a production of shrugging. "Why the hell not? The kid was in a panic after hammering Linville. He probably tossed the iron into a Dumpster or a garbage can. We'll be lucky to ever find it. No doubt it's on a trash barge by now, headed out to sea or wherever they let the things go these days."

"The news reports on Mr. Linville's death suggested that he was killed with a heavy instrument, likely a tire iron that was missing from a collection of tools on the floor near the front doors of the garage," Wolfe remarked.

"What of it?" Cramer snapped.

"Only that Mr. James had sufficient information and details to construct a plausible tale."

"Just a minute, dammit!" Cramer was up out of his chair and leaning on Wolfe's desk with both hands. "You already know that I'd like nothing more than to see the kid be innocent, but there's just too much going against him. We got the right guy."

Wolfe and Cramer locked glares, and then the inspector took a step back from the desk. "What the hell, it's in the D.A.'s hands now anyway," he said, doing a crisp about-face and heading for the hall. Replaying a scene we've both been part of dozens of times, I followed about three paces behind and watched as he went out, slamming the front door behind him.

"He took the cigar with him," I said in wonderment when I was back in the office. "Maybe he finally got tired of missing the wastebasket."

"Mr. Cramer is deeply troubled," Wolfe ventured, ringing for beer.

"Uh-huh. He didn't sound very convincing in saying they had got the right guy. Also, he didn't even bother telling you to butt out this time."

"Miss Rowan will be here at three? And Mr. James at nine?"

"Lily's a for-sure. Right now, James is a maybe, although his sister thinks she can get him to come. He'll be here if I have to drag him by the heels."

"And you have a funeral to attend," Wolfe responded, unimpressed by my chest-thumping.

"I was just leaving, sahib."

TWELVE

The funeral will, of course, be a travesty," Wolfe observed dryly as I was halfway out the office door. "But you know as well as I do that these barbaric ceremonies serve as magnets for all sorts—including murderers."

"Yes sir. You may even be able to catch portions of the travesty right here in the office," I told him, nodding toward the television set. His answer was a scowl.

The service was in one of the big Protestant churches on Fifth Avenue. The day was pleasant, and I had almost an hour so I walked, spotting the travesty from two blocks away. Police barricades were up, limiting traffic to just two lanes, to allow for the funeral procession and the TV stations' mobile units, of which I counted four. Knots of people, many of them shoppers, had begun to form behind ropes on the sidewalk in front of the church, gawking at the celebrities.

Uniformed police manned the ropes, but they did not stop those wanting to enter. I went up the steps, took a leaflet from a somber-looking man with a small, droopy flower in his lapel, and slid into a rear pew on the right side of the old church. I was fifteen minutes early, but already the sanctuary was about three-quarters full, and it could probably hold at least six hundred.

I made a pretense of studying the leaflet, which

turned out to be a program for the service, but my eyes moved over the crowd. I spotted the *Gazette* man right away, Clint Thomas, the paper's best feature writer. I also thought I recognized a woman from the *Times*, but wasn't sure. As for the TV people, they weren't allowed inside—or at least their cameras and lights and sound gear weren't, although several of the video reporters themselves, reduced to using writing implements, undoubtedly were seated.

As the organ began playing, I could feel eyes boring in on me from the left and, sure enough, on the far side of the big room, there was Sergeant Purley Stebbins, standing against a wall and frowning in my direction. I smiled and nodded, getting a deeper frown in reply. I silently mouthed the words "Lighten up, Purley," to which he turned away and continued surveying the assemblage.

I followed suit. It was a well-dressed crowd, as you would expect. Mostly middle-aged, many of them friends and business associates of the parents, although there was a scattering of young men and women of Sparky Linville's generation. At twelve twenty-five the family filed into the first pew from a door up front, where the closed casket was. I recognized Linville's mother and father from the newspapers and television. There was a lot more family, too, enough to fill several pews. A group of eight young men, the pallbearers, marched in from the other side at the front. Halliburton's white hair made him stand out despite his size.

The crimson-robed, curly-headed minister, who seemed surprisingly young, opened with a prayer promptly at ten, and then we rose for a hymn. After that, the minister sermonized, struggling to explain how such an inexplicable event as murder can occur in God's world. There was another hymn, another prayer, and then the pallbearers wheeled the casket down the center aisle and hefted it out the door.

The scene in front of the church was American

because of the natural setting. I had Herb drop me about a hundred yards down the road from the burial site, which was covered by a green canopy. We'd made good time; the procession of limos and other cars—and a few cabs—was still pulling up. I donned my sunglasses and positioned myself inconspicuously, or so I hoped, at the edge of the standees who were gathering.

Again I searched for familiar mugs. Purley was here too, of course, but he didn't even bother to acknowledge me this time. As the graveside service began, I blinked. There, toward the back of the standees on the opposite side of the grave, Edward Pamsett had materialized, and was watching the proceedings intently; he must have had a speedy hack driver of his own. Once again I felt sure he hadn't seen me. And I wasn't about to give him another opportunity. Satisfied that there were no others there of interest, I eased away from the gravesite and the mournful droning of the minister and went back to where Herb was parked, reading the *Daily Racing Form*.

"Back to the land of the living?" he asked, and I nodded grimly. I'd had my quota of cemetery visits for the year.

journalism at its worst. The TV Minicams crowded
so close to the hearse that the pallbearers had
muscle them aside just to roll the casket in. Pr
reporters shouted to Linville's parents as they mov
toward a limousine, trying to get comments, but
uniformed police made like the Giants' offensive li
and in one instance a reporter shoved back, only
get a whack with a nightstick that sent him stagger
and muttering about police brutality.

It took fifteen minutes to get all the VIP gr
loaded into the dozen or so black limos that
lined up behind the hearse. As I stood on the ch
steps surveying the debacle, I spied none other
Edward Pamsett. Clad in a light blue blazer, h
standing toward the rear of the crowd down o
sidewalk, eyes fixed on the hearse. I wondered
had been inside.

As the entourage, led by siren-wailing polic
and six motorcycle escorts, pulled away from the
I took another look at Pamsett, who apparently
seen me, and I slipped away in the opposite dir
I turned into a side street to where a yello
bearing a familiar number and with a famili
behind the wheel idled in a no-parking zone,
DUTY sign lit.

"Right where you're supposed to be," I sa
ing into the back seat.

"You're surprised?" asked Herb Aronson,
dependable taxi driver in the five boroughs.
where you said to be, and when you said to
Question: In twenty years, have I ever fai
Answer: No. Next stop, Long Island, right?"

"Right," I said, and settled back as we he
the cemetery.

The media circus at the cemetery ou
island was a little more subdued than the
chapter. There were as many TV mobile
reporters as before, but they were quiet

THIRTEEN

After Herb dropped me at the brownstone and drove away forty-five dollars healthier, I briefed Wolfe on the funeral, then set about tackling the rest of his instructions from the night before, which were that I pay visits to Noreen's roommate, Polly Mars; her sometime boyfriend, Douglas Rojek; and Todd Halliburton, the stubby garbage-mouth I had the misfortune to have met on the last night of Sparky Linville's life.

I called Noreen at her mother's place again, informing her I wanted to see her roommate, and she said I could usually find Polly in their apartment during the day on weekends unless she went home to see her family in Bronxville. On weekdays, I was told the best time to find her in was around six at night. "That's usually when she gets done with whatever modeling job she has and before she goes out for the evening—and Polly goes out a lot," Noreen said. She didn't sound very excited about my wanting to see Rojek, but she gave me his phone number and address over in Brooklyn. And she couldn't feed me any more about Halliburton than she did before, having met him only twice. She repeated that he lived down in the Village and worked for one of the big insurance companies, or so she thought.

I checked the Manhattan directory and found a Halliburton, T.C., on King Street in the Village, then leaned back and contemplated my course of action, glancing occasionally at Wolfe, who remained motionless and noiseless behind his book. I decided after due reflection that I would call on each of the three at home rather than phoning first, opting for the element of surprise—if indeed there was anything to surprise them with. But because it now was almost two-forty-five, there wasn't time to do much of anything other than sneak out to the kitchen for a quick snack before Lily's arrival at three. I might be able to see one of them, no more, in the late afternoon, leaving two of the visits for Sunday.

So much for the Mets and Cardinals. I had originally asked Saul to go with me, but now I called and inquired as to whether he could use both tickets. He said his friend, the same one who helped pick me clean at the poker table the night before, had decided to stay in town an extra day, so this all worked out very well—for everybody but yours truly. Saul offered to reimburse me, but I told him to consider this as one warm, gregarious New Yorker's gift to an out-of-town visitor. Saul made a choking sound and said he'd be by later to collect the tickets.

Because Wolfe hadn't expressed any preference as to whom I should see first, I decided I would favor Miss Mars with my presence at the earliest opportunity, probably later in the afternoon. I didn't bother sharing my plan with him, however, knowing that he didn't care what order I saw them in.

I'm not sure why Wolfe wanted to see Lily, other than because she is one of the few women he feels comfortable with. This may have something to do with her interest in his orchids, which she has asked to see at least a couple of dozen times through the years, and to my knowledge, she has yet to get a turndown.

Anyway, Wolfe's conversation with Lily did little other than reinforce what he already had learned from Noreen and from what I had reported to him: namely, that both Noreen and Michael James were upstanding, moral, clean-cut, and essentially decent young specimens, although Michael was prone both to stuffiness and to bursts of temper; and that Sparky Linville was crude, boorish, and generally disagreeable.

Wolfe managed to stretch the conversation for an hour, and I knew why: He fully expected Lily to ask to visit the orchids, which she hadn't seen for a while, and she didn't disappoint him. So when he left the office at four to go to the plant rooms, he wasn't alone.

"You two kids have a great time with the posies," I told Wolfe and Lily as the elevator door started to close. I got a glower from him and a wink from her, then went to the kitchen to inform Fritz that I likely would be gone until dinnertime.

The Noreen James–Polly Mars apartment in the West Eighties was in a four-story building that had known better times. My watch told me it was four-thirty-three when I got out of a cab, walked up the stone steps into the small vestibule, and rang the bell next to the nameplate that said MARS–JAMES 3-W. I waited fifteen seconds, cursed in a whisper, and rang again. This time I was rewarded with a static-riddled "Yes?"

"Archie Goodwin—I'm a friend of your room-mate, Noreen," I said, leaning close to the speaker and talking both slowly and loudly. A lady passing by on the sidewalk with a white poodle stopped and stared at me.

"I don't know you," came the crisp response, to which I suggested she call Noreen at her mother's apartment, hoping I was understood through the archaic intercom.

I waited two minutes, three, five, and then I

heard something that sounded like "Okay" rasp through the speaker, followed by a click that released the door. The walk up two dark, narrow flights that smelled of disinfectant confirmed my initial impression of the building. At 3-W I knocked and identified myself, getting another muffled "Okay" from within. The door opened as far as the chain would allow, and I saw one slice of what looked to be a well-arranged face.

"You're Archie Goodwin?" the slice asked. "May I see identification?" I pulled out my laminated private investigator's license, which has my picture on it, and held it close. "All right, you're you," Polly Mars said, swinging the door open and revealing that the whole face was well-arranged indeed. Noreen hadn't exaggerated her roommate's beauty. "I'm sorry to have taken so long, but, well, you have to be careful, you know. Also, I just finished washing my hair when you rang," she said, gesturing toward the white towel coiled atop her head that hid all but a few strands of very blond hair. "Please come in. And sit down."

The living room wasn't overly large, but it was nicely furnished—a pleasant surprise after the front of the building and the hallway. Music—it sounded like something from an opera—was playing softly. I parked on a comfortable-looking beige sofa while Polly Mars, wearing blue jeans, a loose white blouse, and sneakers, sat in a wing chair at my right. "I just phoned Noreen, like you said," she told me. "She said you wanted to talk about Sparky and everything, and she also said that it was okay to answer whatever you asked. Isn't it terrible about her brother being arrested and all?" She talked with her long manicured fingers, moving them with each syllable.

"Yes, it is, Miss Mars. When did you find out about the arrest?"

More hand fluttering. "Oh, just now, from Noreen. She's really upset. I suppose it's been in the papers and all, but I never seem to get around to reading them, although I know I should. She told me you and Nero Wolfe are trying to prove Michael didn't . . . do it."

"That's right. First off, I'd like your thoughts on why Michael James would want to kill Mr. Linville."

Polly sucked on her lower lip and let her eyes move around the room, as if she were thinking. She had some stagy mannerisms, for sure, but you could probably chalk that up to her modeling. It was easy to imagine her peddling toothpaste on TV. "Well, I . . . I don't know."

"Remember Noreen's words—that it is okay to answer any question I ask," I said with a smile.

She tucked one leg under her and frowned, as if responding to a cue. "Well, I guess you know that Noreen went out with Sparky, don't you?" I nodded. "Something went wrong, it was on their second date. She didn't talk to me about it, but I could tell," she said.

"How?"

"She got really withdrawn, you know? She didn't talk hardly at all for days. I was visiting my parents that weekend—they live up in Bronxville—and when I came back here, she was like a different person. Quieter—a lot quieter. And one thing was for sure—she didn't want to see Sparky anymore."

"Did she give you any reason?"

"No." She shook her head vigorously, nearly dislodging the towel. "I asked her why she wouldn't talk to him when he called, and she just said she wasn't interested anymore. Then I asked her if anything went wrong, and she said no. I really felt guilty that things had gone bad, because she met Sparky through me."

"I'd like to hear how that happened."

Polly wrinkled her nose and fidgeted some more, then fixed her hazel eyes on me as if to come forth with a revelation. "I don't know if Noreen told you this, but I had gone out with Sparky a few times myself, and one night when we came back here for a drink after we'd been out, he met Noreen."

"Interesting. How well would you say you knew Linville?"

"Oh, we had a few dates. He was a lot of fun, knew a lot of people." Her long fingers were flying again as she talked.

"The newspapers made him sound like he was more than a tad on the wild side."

"Well, he loved to drive fast, too fast, I suppose, and he liked to hit all the hot spots, but he was really okay." She mouthed it without conviction.

"Back to Noreen. What's your opinion as to what happened between her and Linville?"

This time I got both nose-wrinkling and eye-rolling. "I don't know. Maybe he put some moves on her or something."

"Was that typical of him?"

Polly blushed and this time didn't bother with the dramatics. "I really wouldn't know," she replied stiffly.

"You can do better than that," I said, easing forward and leaning on my knees. "One man is dead, another has been charged with his murder, and your roommate is devastated. This is no time for getting coy. I know this is sensitive stuff, but to use a cliché, a life may be on the line. Now, tell me about you and Sparky Linville."

She did, and it wasn't at all pretty. She deserves more than a modicum of privacy, however, so I will only report that her own unpleasant experience with Linville—also on their final date—was not unlike Noreen's. Tears came early on in her narrative, and by the end she was sobbing into the handkerchief I had passed to her.

"Miss Mars, I promise you none of this will ever get beyond Mr. Wolfe and me unless it is absolutely vital to establish an individual's innocence or guilt. But I must ask one more tough question: Given your own experience with Linville, how could you let Noreen James go out with him?"

She moaned and sniffled into the handkerchief before raising a tearstained face. "Oh, God, that's the worst part of all. I couldn't bear to tell anybody what happened to me—not my parents, not Noreen, not even my shrink. And I'm a better actor than Noreen is; I kept it hidden. Also, one thing I didn't mention: Sparky had gotten interested in Noreen before . . . before what happened to me. He even asked me—this was before our last date, if you want to call it that—he asked me if I minded his calling her."

"And?"

"And I told him no, I didn't mind, which was true. I was never serious about Sparky, I just like to have a good time, and he knew how to have a good time. I mean, you know, not like what—"

"Yes, I know what you mean," I said solemnly. "So it was after your episode with him that he asked Noreen to go out?"

"Yes!" she spat it angrily, dabbing at her eyes. "After Noreen told me he'd called her, she wanted to know if I had any objections, and I was flabbergasted. I stuttered around and at least said one true thing—that I wasn't interested in Sparky. I was so damn stupid. I wish I'd said more to her. Anyway, when Noreen wasn't around, I phoned Sparky and told him to stay the hell away from her. I said if he didn't, I was going to tell her what happened to me."

"His reaction?"

"He said nothing happened to me that I didn't want to have happen. And then he laughed—he *laughed*. He told me that I'd never say anything about it to anybody because that would make me look bad, and he said that not looking bad was more important to me than anything else. And dammit, maybe he was right. Mr. Goodwin, I hated him for what he did to me, I hated him for what he did to Noreen, and I hated myself most of all for not warning her about him." Her tears had turned to rage. "God, I'm such a coward."

"Easy," I said, putting a hand on her arm. "How close are you and Noreen?"

"We went to college together and we've been roommates here for two years. But even with all that, we don't talk much about, well . . . the *really* personal stuff, if you know what I mean."

That confirmed what Noreen had told me. "I do. What do you think occurred between Noreen and Linville?"

She wrung my damp handkerchief nervously. "Huh. That's obvious. She never told me, but she didn't have to. I could tell from the way she acted. And even knowing that, I didn't try to comfort her. Some friend I am, all the way around!"

"So here you were, two roommates with apparently identical experiences, and nobody said a thing—to each other or to anyone else?"

Polly nodded soberly. I wondered how many others, like her and Noreen, were locked in self-imposed prisons of silence because of similar horrors. Far more than those who spoke out against their attackers, I supposed. "Miss Mars," I said gently, "I'm sure you know Michael James. What is your opinion about his arrest?"

"How do you mean?"

"Do you think he killed Linville?"

She twitched her shoulders twice, then raised her dewy eyes. I'd buy toothpaste from her any day. "I don't know Michael terribly well—oh, I've met him a few times, although we never talked a lot to each other. But, yeah, I guess it wouldn't surprise me at all that he did it."

"Any particular reason for saying that?"

"Mr. Goodwin, I've got an older brother too—his name is Chris—and if he ever found out what had happened to me, like Michael must have found out with Noreen, I honestly think he would have gone berserk and killed Sparky, too."

"Miss Mars," I said, watching her face carefully, "where were you on Wednesday night?"

"Wednesday night? Let's see, I was . . . Wait a minute, why do you want to know?" She recoiled, realizing where I was coming from.

"Why *wouldn't* I want to know?"

"So you think I'm the one who . . ." She let it trail off, looking at me reproachfully.

"I didn't say that, but in fact, you must admit you had a reason for intensely disliking Linville."

"And now you know that reason."

'You still haven't answered the question," I said.

She readjusted the towel with a hand, letting it come to rest on her right cheek, then punched up her reproachful look, obviously hoping I would say something to make her feel better or else let her off the hook. I kept my mouth shut and my face expressionless and waited.

"Wednesday night," she repeated dully. "I was . . . I had a late photo assignment, in a studio on East Fifty-second."

"How late?"

"Until . . . about seven-thirty."

"Then what?"

"I had dinner at a little Italian place on Sixth Avenue up near the park."

"Alone?"

"Yes," she said. "I got out of there about nine and took a cab back here."

"Again, alone?"

"Yes. Nobody was here. Noreen was staying at her mother's place, but you probably know that."

"And the rest of the evening?"

"I stayed home, watched a little TV, did some ironing, went to bed around eleven. I guess I don't have an alibi, do I, for when Sparky got killed?" she said in what she tried to make a defiant tone.

"I guess not."

"Except that Michael James already has confessed," she went on, not sounding the least bit satisfied about it. "Mr. Goodwin, it's hard to blame him for what he did. I just hope that he doesn't have to pay for this in any way. Now, *that* would really be a crime. As far as I'm concerned, Michael James is a real hero. If it were up to me, I'd give him a medal."

FOURTEEN

Polly Mars was still on her soapbox trumpeting
Michael James as the Great American Avenger
when I left her apartment. I did stay around long
enough to see her pull herself together, helped by a
shot of brandy I poured from an unopened bottle she
and Noreen kept in a kitchen cabinet, and I reassured
her that her story would go no further than the brownstone unless absolutely necessary. "Do whatever it takes
to help Michael," were her parting words as I left and
descended the dark hallways to the street, where light
rain was now falling. Miraculously, I landed a cab in
less than a half-minute, which meant I got home in
plenty of time to clean up, take a twenty-minute catnap, and put on a fresh shirt before sitting down to a
dinner of capon Souvaroff.

Fritz's capon was so good that it almost made me
forget we had a nine-o'clock business engagement. It
came back to me when Wolfe and I were in the office
with coffee, though, and he asked for a fill-in on my
visit with Polly. I gave him the usual verbatim of the
conversation as he leaned back, eyes closed and fingers interlaced over his middle mound. After I finished he made no comment, but did ring for beer.

It was ten after nine when the front doorbell
rang. Peering out through the one-way glass, I saw a
frowning Noreen James standing in the rain on the
stoop with a dark-haired, square-shouldered, square-
jawed young man I took to be her brother. He had

what I would label a pleasant, honest face, but at least at that moment it totally lacked animation. "Come in," I said in my best host's voice, pulling the door toward me and stepping aside.

"Mr. Goodwin—I mean Archie, I'm sorry we're late; we had a horrific time getting a cab, what with the rain and all," Noreen said, shaking her umbrella. "This is my brother, Michael." She smiled weakly while I hung up his raincoat and offered him a paw, which was returned firmly but without enthusiasm or words. Michael wore gray slacks, a white open-collared sport shirt, and a light blue sport coat, and he looked like he'd rather be just about anyplace but where he was.

"I know I'm not even supposed to be here," Noreen half-whispered in the front hall, her eyes jumping from Michael to me and back again like she was watching a tennis match. "Where do you want me to go?"

"Come into the office first, then we'll get you settled in the front room," I told her with a smile, steering both of them toward a meeting with Wolfe. He gave us a bland expression as we walked in, setting his book down and leaning back. I introduced Michael, directing him to the red leather chair, then escorted Noreen to the front room, where, I told her, Fritz would soon arrive to look after her refreshment needs. I then made with a quick detour to the kitchen to tell Fritz our female guest warranted a visit.

I got back to the office just as Wolfe was starting in. "Mr. James, you're in a pickle. However—"

"Look," Michael said, sticking out his dandy chin and running a hand through thick, curly hair, "I'm only here because my sister begged me to come, really begged me. I couldn't believe it when I heard she had hired you. I mean, for God's sake, I killed the . . ." He paused, groping for a noun, then pronounced it with relish.

"So I sit in the company of a murderer," Wolfe intoned softly, placing an index finger on the side of his nose. "As long as you already are here, however, I would be interested, given my profession, in what impelled you to this action."

Michael looked puzzled. "Wait a minute—Noreen told me you knew all about everything," he blurted.

"She discussed various facets of what I choose to term her incident with Mr. Linville," Wolfe said. "But at the moment I am interested in your own perspective on the events."

"Huh!" Michael tugged at his belt and arranged his smooth, strong face into a sour smile. "The jerk—Linville, that is—he, well . . . *you* know what he did."

"I know what I have been told he did. How did you learn of this?"

"I hadn't seen Nor for a few weeks," Michael muttered belligerently. "Then, when Mother got home from France, we had a get-together to welcome her back, and it was obvious that Nor was . . . well, she looked like hell. Anyway, Mother didn't take long—that's the way she is—to learn exactly what happened. I mean with Linville. That's when we all found out." Michael leaned back and turned his palms up, as though that explained everything.

"So you, being the noble sibling, exacted the ultimate vengeance?"

Michael scowled at Wolfe, lowering the brows over his dark eyes. "Listen, nobody messes with my sister without answering to me."

"Boldly said, sir. Did you inform anyone outside of the family circle of what had happened to your sister?"

"Well, in a way," he answered tentatively, allowing his eyes to move around the room.

"Oh?"

"The next day, I sort of mentioned something about it to Doug Rojek—he's a guy I know down on Wall Street, maybe Nor told you about him. They've gone out a fair amount the last few months."

"How did you 'sort of mention' something to him?" Wolfe asked.

Michael slouched in the chair. "Well, I had lunch with him in Battery Park—a couple of times a week we get a soda and a hot dog and eat them on a bench. Anyway, I guess it just sort of came out when we talked. I was still really hot about it and . . . hell, I know I shouldn't have said anything to him, but I did. For God's sake, please don't tell Nor."

"How did Mr. Rojek react to this revelation?" Wolfe probed, ignoring the entreaty.

"He got, well, real quiet, didn't say anything for the rest of the lunch. I started to wish I hadn't opened my big mouth. I guess it really depressed him."

"Did you share with him any plans you had regarding Mr. Linville?"

"God, no, Doug didn't have anything to do with what happened," Michael said tensely. "This was my thing, and why in the hell my mother and father want to spend a fortune on a lawyer for me is more than I can figure. Same with Nor wanting to spend another fortune getting you to try to—"

Wolfe cut him off sharply. "Exactly when did you plot Mr. Linville's demise?" he snapped.

"I guess from the minute I heard what he did to Nor. Although at first, I didn't plan to kill him, just rough him up good, mess up that smirky face, you know?"

"When did assault turn to murder in your mind?" Wolfe asked.

He shrugged. "I dunno. I suppose when I followed him and that damn Porsche of his into the garage and spotted the tire iron on the floor."

"You were stalking him at the time?"

"If you want to call it that. I had gone around to a few bars and places where he hung around."

"Had you met him before?"

"No—although I'd seen him in Orion three or

four times. He was hard to miss. He was always the loudest guy anyplace he went."

Wolfe paused to sip his beer, then asked Michael if he wanted anything to drink. The answer was a shake of the head.

"Did you know before this week that Mr. Linville had had social engagements with your sister?"

"Dammit, no! If I had, I would have stopped it right then," he growled, making a fist and shaking it at a nonexistent target.

"Oh?" Wolfe raised his eyebrows. "Is Miss James accustomed to having you dictate to her in that manner?"

Older brother sat upright and gave Wolfe another one of his low-eyebrow looks, then turned toward me. He got only my blandest expression. He swung back toward Wolfe, tight-lipped. "Okay, maybe she would have listened to me, maybe she wouldn't. But at least I'd have had my say about that . . . jerk." I knew he had any one of several stronger words in mind, but he settled for a tame one.

"Mr. James," Wolfe said with a sigh, "what did you say to Mr. Linville before you dispatched him?"

"God, you know, I've been through all this with the cops, Cramer, and the others."

"I appreciate that, sir. But I ask your indulgence. The police are not accustomed to sharing their information with Mr. Goodwin and me."

"Okay," Michael said, kneading his hands. "I saw Linville drive into the garage where he parks and—"

"Excuse me, but I'm curious as to how far that garage is from Mr. Linville's building."

"How far? Hell, it's about three, maybe four doors west," Michael snapped irritably.

"Had you known that was where he kept his automobile?"

"I . . . No, I didn't. Why?"

"Then how did you happen to be there when he arrived?" Wolfe asked.

"It was . . . just good timing."

"Or bad timing," Wolfe remarked dryly, eyes on the ceiling. "So you followed him into the garage on foot?"

"You got it," Michael said. "And it looks like I'm going to have a lot of time to think about what I did once I got in there, doesn't it?"

"Indeed. Tell me again, please, about the tire iron."

"What's to tell? It was on the floor, just inside the big door, which Linville had unlocked before he drove in. The door was still up when I walked in behind him, and I just spotted it among a pile of tools."

"What other tools were there?"

Michael's forehead wrinkled. "It was dark, but I think a jack, some wrenches, and at least one of those four-sided things to take lugs off a tire, and . . . well, that's all I noticed."

"Understandable," Wolfe said. "After all, as you say, it *was* dark. And now, a hypothetical question, if you don't mind: Let us assume for a moment that there had been no tools piled inside the door, no tire iron. How do you think you would have proceeded against Mr. Linville in that situation?"

"I probably would have popped him a few times, but I did some boxing in college, so even my punches might have killed him," Michael said in a smug tone.

"But you reached for the tire iron, with specific intent to use it?"

"Damn right," Michael shot back. "And I'm not sorry."

"Evidently. Did you engage Mr. Linville in conversation before you delivered the coup de grace?"

"As he was getting out of the car, I hollered to him—I called his name. He looked at me, sort of puzzled. I mean, he'd never met me before, although I'd seen *him* a couple times around town, like in Orion. Anyway, I walked up to him and said my name. It didn't register, so then I told him I was Nor's brother, and he gave me a funny smile, like he was all of a sudden figuring things out."

"Did he appear to be intoxicated?" Wolfe asked.

"Hard to tell. Maybe. Anyway, he started to laugh, and that's when I lost it and called him a bastard and swung the tire iron. I don't even know how many times I hit him." His expression was impassive.

Wolfe drank beer, then set his glass down, frowning at it. "What was Mr. Linville wearing?"

"What does that have to do with anything?" Michael snarled.

"Just my curiosity," Wolfe said. "What did you do after striking him down?"

Michael fidgeted irritably. "Like I said, I've told all this to the cops already. I ran out the door."

"Where did you go?"

"Home."

"Via what route?"

"I went west on Seventy-seventh and caught a cab on Second Avenue."

"What about the tire iron?"

"Like I told the cops, Cramer and the others, I thought I dropped it in the garage, but I honestly can't remember. But they say they didn't find it in the garage, so maybe I carried it with me."

"To Second Avenue?" Wolfe asked.

"All I know is that I didn't have it with me when I got into the damn cab. Everything is kind of hazy about that time, you know. Look, the lawyer they got for me doesn't want me to talk to anyone, and the only reason I'm even here is because of Noreen. I know you've got a reputation as some kind of genius, but that's not going to do me any good. Face it, I'm dead meat."

Wolfe eyed our visitor for several seconds without stirring. "Sir, you may indeed be, as you term it, 'dead meat.' And my services may patently be superfluous. Your sister, however, seems unswerving in her conviction of your innocence."

"What would you expect of a sister?" Michael asked, smiling sourly. "I mean, she's not about to hang me out to dry."

"But you appear more than willing to hang yourself out to dry," Wolfe remarked.

"What can I say? I bashed the guy, and I'm not sorry about it. He did something—all three of us here know exactly what it was—and then I did something. I'd do it all over again, with a tire iron, or with my hands, or with anything else I could find. Now, I know guys like you make out big on retainers, which is fine, I guess. And I also know that Nor can afford you, but she's wasting her time. Give her back her money, and I'll pay you the same amount, and then you can drop all of this because, believe me, it's hopeless. They got the right guy."

"Mr. James, yours is not an unattractive proposal," Wolfe conceded. "Indeed, given certain circumstances, I might be inclined to consider such an offer, but I must in this situation respectfully decline."

"What's the matter—don't you believe I have the money?" Michael challenged.

"On the contrary, Mr. James. I don't doubt for a moment that you do."

"Then what's the problem? You said under certain circumstances, you'd be—what?—'inclined to consider the offer,' I think, is the way you put it. What the hell are the circumstances?"

Wolfe readjusted his bulk. "Borrowing loosely from the language of the Bible, the first and great circumstance under which I would ponder such a proposition is if its giver were guilty. And you, sir, are manifestly not guilty."

Michael James started to get up, glared at Wolfe, who glared back, and then sat down again. "Listen, Wolfe, you may be a genius, but you've blown it this time. Do you mean to say that even with me admitting to offing Linville, you guys are going to go ahead and take my sister's money? I think that stinks."

I must interrupt here to report that "stinks" is not the word young James used, but my practice is to keep these narratives relatively free from what Wolfe has referred to as "the desecration of the language." So "stinks" will have to do, and if you think another word works better, feel free to make the substitution—you might even be correct.

Anyway, after Wolfe got told off, he looked at James and sniffed. "I am of the opinion that your sister is firmly in the possession of her faculties. Were I a charlatan, she would doubtless see through me in an instant and react accordingly. However, you may wish to share your analysis of my motives with her."

"You're damn right I will," Michael yapped, this time getting up in earnest. "Where is she?"

I steered him toward the front room, leaving Wolfe to his devices—which is to say, beer and a book—and ushered him down the hall to the front room, opening it ahead of him. Noreen popped to her feet as he entered, and brother and sister just looked at each other for several seconds.

I finally broke the spell, telling them they were free to remain in the front room and discuss the situation together. I think Noreen would have stayed, but Michael was in no mood to hang around the brownstone for another minute. The rain had stopped, but the smell of dampness was in the air as he hustled her out the front door and down the steps to the street. She turned back to me with an "I'm-sorry-but-that's-Michael-for-you" look as I stood in the doorway.

"Well, what do you think of our young suspect?" I asked Wolfe back in the office.

"Pah. The man is as diaphane as a pane of plate glass," he huffed.

"Uh-huh. If he ever set foot in that garage, then I'm a nuclear physicist."

Wolfe made a face at my phrasing and opened his new book, *A Brief History of Time*, by Stephen W. Hawking. For him, the working day, such as it was, had ended, and I was in no mood to badger him any further. After all, I already had my assignments for tomorrow, and he was just perverse enough to cancel them if I became what he terms an insufferable nuisance.

FIFTEEN

On Sundays, the brownstone's by-the-numbers schedule gets a breather. For Fritz, it's a free day, although sometimes he stays around and he and Wolfe whip up something together for lunch. More often, though, he takes off, leaving His Largeness free to run amok in the kitchen, where he actually prepares his own meals on what is for him a haphazard timetable. The plant-room schedule also flies out the window. Theodore usually visits his sister in New Jersey for the day, and Wolfe may make one or even two random voyages to the roof to putter. But he spends most of the day lazing in the chair at his desk, wrestling with the Sunday *Times*, particularly the "Week in Review" section and the magazine, whose crossword puzzle is no match for him.

My day is likewise generally unstructured. I also do a bit of improvising in the kitchen, at least in the morning, and after plowing through my own copy of the *Times*, I've been known to amble over to Lily's penthouse. Sometimes the two of us have lunch at her place and dinner out, other times we reverse the procedure or maybe go to a concert or a ballgame. And when Lily isn't available, I wing it, as I thought I was doing by taking in the Mets double-header with Saul. But you already know what happened to that plan.

Actually, I'm not averse to working Sundays because, whatever faults I find with Wolfe, he is flexible

regarding time off, and he has mellowed to where he
feels a Sunday spent toiling is worth two days of
freedom at another time. All of which helps make it
possible for me to occasionally escape with Lily to her
not-so-humble country place up near Katonah for
extra-long weekends without eating into my vacation
time.

I decided to tackle Douglas Rojek first on that
overcast Sabbath morning. It was just past eleven when,
after having consumed scrambled eggs, link sausage,
whole-wheat toast, orange juice, two cups of coffee,
and all I wanted of the *Times*, I stood up from my
desk, stretched, and announced to Wolfe that I was
about to venture forth on behalf of the Family James.
He grunted an acknowledgment but did not look up
from the paper, so I made a witty remark about not
being appreciated and slipped on my suit coat, re-
minding him to bolt the door behind me. After all,
Wolfe has made enough enemies through the years to
fill Madison Square Garden, and a goodly number
undoubtedly know our address.

The day was pleasantly cool for late July in New
York, and it looked like rain again. I briefly considered getting the Mercedes from the garage for the
trip across the East River, but decided in favor of a
cab, which I hailed on Eighth Avenue. The driver
balked at going to Brooklyn Heights, but when I
asked his name and started writing his license number
in my notebook, he growled for me to get in, and we
drove through the nearly empty streets in silence,
which suited me fine.

Twenty-two minutes and one bridge later, I found
myself on a hilly tree-lined block that could be termed
gentrified, which is real-estate shorthand for expensive. The buildings on both sides were three- and
four-story brownstones, and they all looked as if they
had been given a face lift in the last few years. There
were no children in sight, hardly a surprise considering the neighborhood's prices.

Rojek's building was a three-story number, every bit as nice as any on the block, and judging by the name on the mailbox in the foyer, he lived alone, in 2-N. The young man either came from money or was doing very well indeed across the river in Wall Street's canyons. I rang his bell and got another squawky "Yes?" through the speaker. When I told the voice I was a friend of Noreen James, I was promptly buzzed in. I climbed the wallpapered stairwell to the third floor, where a thin face wearing a quizzical expression peered from behind a partly open door. "What do you want?" it asked.

"Are you Douglas Rojek?" I said with what I hoped was a friendly, nonthreatening voice to go with my most earnest smile.

"Yes. Who are you?" The door came open a little farther and I could see earnestness, although without a smile, looking back at me in the form of a long face with prominent cheekbones topped by sandy hair that spilled over one side of a high forehead. He wore khaki pants and a blue button-down shirt open at the collar. A college ring with a dark blue stone gleamed from his finger.

"My name is Archie Goodwin, and I am in the employ of Nero Wolfe, of whom you may have heard. Mr. Wolfe is investigating the death of Barton Linville, and his client is Noreen—"

"Noreen?" he cut in, shaking his head. "I . . . Oh, come in, come in. I can't get over what's happened." He directed me into a good-sized, light living room furnished with some pricey contemporary pieces. The Sunday *Times* was stacked in two neat piles on the floor. "Please, sit down," he said, gesturing toward the sofa and moving his angular frame to a chair. Douglas Rojek was all of six-three, but if he weighed one-sixty, it would have to be with all his clothes on, including a fur-lined overcoat and thick-soled boots.

"All right, Mr. . . . Goodwin, isn't it?" Rojek hunched his shoulders and shifted nervously as he sat with his legs wide apart. "Tell me what's happening. I've seen the papers and watched the TV news, of course, and I've tried to phone Noreen, but her mother answers and says she can't be disturbed. And Michael—he's, what, out on bond? God, I just can't believe any of this is happening. It's incredible. A nightmare." He shook his head and yanked a cigarette pack from his pocket, lighting up with a match and offering me one, which I declined.

"It certainly seems like a nightmare to all the Jameses," I agreed. "You know Michael well, very well from what I gather. Do you think he's capable of murder? Specifically, of murdering Sparky Linville?"

"Well . . . the papers are saying he did it because of . . . well, something that happened between him—Linville, I mean—and Noreen." Rojek kept his eyes on the stack of business magazines on the glass coffee table.

"I know what the papers are saying. I want to know what *you* think."

Rojek ground out his cigarette in the ashtray although it was barely a third smoked, then ran a long-fingered hand over his face and chin. "I don't know what to think. At this point, the whole thing is more than I can understand."

"How would you describe your relationship with Noreen James?"

He went through the cigarette-lighting ritual again. "A terrific person," he said. "But then, I don't have to tell you that; you know her."

"I do indeed. Right now, though, we're talking about you and her."

He took a long drag and watched the smoke waft toward the ceiling. He was apparently one of those who'd seen too many Bogart movies, which was all right—so was I. I waited, knowing the pressure was building; I was prepared to give him thirty seconds, but as it turned out, twenty was enough.

"I'm really awfully fond of Noreen," he said self-consciously. "We've gone out quite a lot the last few months, and . . ."

"And?"

Rojek let his bony shoulders bounce a couple of times. "And we get along wonderfully," he said as though he meant it. "Wonderfully."

"So let's go back to Michael. Do you think he killed Linville?"

He shook his head. "I really don't know. It's hard for me to believe, but . . ." He turned his palms up.

I was done fooling around. "Mr. Rojek," I said, "precisely what do you know about the relationship between Barton Linville and Noreen James?"

He stubbed out another cigarette and frowned at the ashtray. "I know they went out a couple of times or so," he said, spacing the words. "But that was Noreen's business."

"Did it bother you?"

More shoulder bouncing. "Oh, I guess so, but after all, I have no particular claim on her. She's free to do whatever she wants."

"That's noble, Mr. Rojek. Did you have any long-range plans involving Noreen James?"

"You mean like marriage?"

"Whatever."

"Well . . . *yes*, dammit. I mean, I'd thought about it."

"Did she know that?"

"You're getting awfully personal," he said stiffly.

"The police are likely to get a lot more personal if they talk to you," I said. "Let's quit dancing around the subject. When did you find out what had happened to Noreen?"

This time Rojek looked at the floor rather than the coffee table, rubbing his hands together between his long legs. "Michael told me in so many words when we were having lunch," he muttered.

"And your reaction?"

"I don't know. Stunned, I suppose. Not that something like that couldn't happen to anybody, you know, but . . ." He looked up at me, his Adam's apple bobbing as he swallowed. "Is Noreen okay?"

"She's fine, probably better than you are at this moment. So you knew what had happened to her while Linville was still alive?"

That one took a while to sink in, and he didn't field it particularly well when he did answer. "I guess I did, yeah, I suppose. But so what? What does that mean?"

"Just an observation. When was the last time you talked to Miss James?"

Rojek screwed up his face. "Like I told you, I've tried to call her the last few days."

"What about before that, before Linville was killed?"

Maybe the guy was twitchy all the time, but I doubted it as I watched him brush his hair out of his eyes and scratch his cheek and then his chin, and then make another pass at his hair. "I don't feel, well, *comfortable*, discussing this, you know? I mean, talking about Noreen this way."

"Suit yourself. Chances are, though, that you'll eventually have to talk to somebody, as in the New York police."

"Why?"

"Because Michael James did not murder Sparky Linville. Believe it."

Rojek locked his elbows onto his knees and looked at the dirty carpet below, head in hands. "All right," he said without conviction, looking at me and inhaling twice, as if the room lacked oxygen, "I haven't been with Noreen a whole lot for a couple weeks. She . . . hasn't really wanted to talk to me—or see me, for that matter."

"Care to speculate on the reason?"

"I think it goes back to when she and Linville . . . You know. Michael told me it happened . . . what,

God, about a month ago? That would have been about the time Noreen started . . . avoiding me."

I watched Rojek without saying anything, which made him even more self-conscious. Finally he jerked to his feet and jammed his hands into his pants pockets. "God, so what happens now?" he said plaintively, giving me his back and looking out the window onto the Brooklyn street.

"What happens is you tell me where you were late last Wednesday night and in Thursday's early hours."

He spun around, hands still in his pockets, and leaned toward me, squinting. "That's a tacky thing to say, really cheap."

"I guess that makes me both tacky and cheap then," I told him, standing so that we were more or less on the same level. Like Wolfe, I don't like to have to crane my neck to maintain eye contact. "Look, Mr. Rojek, I admit that you don't have to tell me a damn thing; I'm only a private investigator. But I do know a number of members of the New York Police Department fairly well. Now, that's in no way meant to be a threat, but—"

"But that's exactly what it is," Rojek muttered, letting himself drop back into the chair and pulling out another cigarette, which he didn't light. "We both know I don't have to tell you a thing, but I will," he said, his voice suddenly gone icy. "On Wednesday nights, I always play softball, in a park near here. That's what I did this week too. Lots of people can vouch for me."

"You play your games on a lighted field?" I asked, also sitting again.

"Not us. It's just an after-work league, nothing fancy."

"So you were done before nine?"

He shrugged. "About quarter of, I suppose. I wasn't bothering to check my watch."

"Which means the night was still young."

"That's right," he snapped, looking at his cigarette. "And then about six of us went to a local bar, like we always do after a game. Want the name of the place?"

"Maybe later. How long were you there?"

"An hour, maybe a little more. I had a grand total of two beers, like I usually do."

"And then?"

"And then, Mr. Goodwin, I came back here, read for a while, and went to bed—alone. So I have no alibi at all. Anything else you want to know?"

"Nice place you've got," I observed, looking around. "Live here by yourself?"

"That's right."

"You must do well."

"Yes, I do pretty well," Rojek said, standing again and pressing his lips together. He tossed the unlit cigarette into the ashtray. "And also, although God knows it's no business of yours, I have generous parents. Now, if you don't mind—"

"Hey, say no more," I told him, smiling and holding up a hand. "I know when I've overstayed my welcome, and I have a suspicion that's what I may have done here. But you'd better be prepared for more knocks on your door in the near future, from the police or—who knows?—maybe even from me again."

I didn't get an answer, nor did I expect one. Mr. Personality went to the door without a word and held it open for me. I walked out, giving him one last smile and getting a sneer in return. He wasn't happy, but then, in this business, it's hard to leave 'em laughing.

SIXTEEN

Back out on the street I looked around, wondering how easy it would be to find a taxi in Brooklyn at a little past noon on a Sunday. I walked three blocks to the nearest busy thoroughfare, Flatbush Avenue, and my luck held as a yellow swerved to the curb. Less than fifteen minutes later I found myself on King Street in the Village, just west of Sixth Avenue. The block had good-size trees and was similar to Rojek's neighborhood except all of the buildings here were brick and some were still undergoing gentrification. At least two were gutted and had scaffolding clinging to their facades.

Todd Halliburton lived in a four-story number that looked to have already gone through the upgrading process. As in the case of Rojek, he apparently lived alone on the top floor, at least according to the mailbox. I leaned on the call button, got no response, and hit it again with the same result. Two out of three still isn't bad, I thought as I went down the steps to the sidewalk, noodling over whether to stake the place out or find some food.

My stomach won the debate hands-down, and at twelve-forty I was parked on a stool in a second-rate lunch counter on Sixth Avenue drinking second-rate coffee and eating peach pie. The pie actually was respectable to the degree that I ordered a second piece, checking my watch. It had been forty minutes since I left Halliburton's—time for another try. I dialed his number at the pay phone near the door and on the third ring got a hoarse "Hello?" I hung up, scolding myself for not being patient enough to keep watch on King Street. Now I would have to talk my way into his apartment from the foyer, which figured to be harder than in the cases of Polly Mars and Rojek. As I walked back from the diner, I turned over possible approaches, settling on one that seemed to have a fair chance of success.

This time when I pressed the button, I got a response that sounded roughly like "Whosit?"

"A college buddy of Sparky's," I said, pitching my voice an octave high. The buzzer sounded, and I climbed my third apartment-building staircase of the weekend. This case was going to keep me slim. At the fourth-floor landing I saw a door ajar, and as I neared it, Todd Halliburton, all five-feet-five, pulled it open.

"Hi, what's . . . You!" he yelped, his eyebrows climbing halfway up his forehead. He tried to slam the door, but my foot was too fast and I wedged it between the door and the jamb. "What the hell do you want?" he cried, trying to push me out.

"To see you for a few minutes," I said, forcing the door farther open, muscling him backward and working my way into the apartment.

"If you don't get out of here, I'm calling the police." He retreated into his living room.

"Go ahead," I told him, grinning. "I can give you the number and tell you who to ask for. Actually, you'll be saving them some trouble, because they'll be wanting to talk to you before long anyway."

"What in the hell are you talking about?" He stopped backing up and put his hands on his hips defiantly. He was wearing tennis shorts and one of those powder-puff-colored short-sleeved pullover shirts with a swamp creature glued on where a pocket should be.

"I'm talking about the murder of your friend Linville."

"Well, they got the guy, didn't they? It was on TV and in the papers. Thank God."

"They got *a* guy," I corrected. "But not the right one. Or maybe I should say not the right guy *or* woman."

"Says who?"

"Says Nero Wolfe," I answered quietly. "And when Mr. Wolfe talks, the police listen." Okay, so I was indulging in hyperbole, but given my audience, it seemed apt—and effective.

"So let me get this straight," Halliburton said, head cocked to one side and hands still on hips. "Nero Wolfe—that's your boss, I know—says Michael James didn't kill Sparky? What kind of bull is that? The paper said he confessed."

"Don't believe everything you read. Mind if I sit?"

He obviously minded, but for the moment, anyway, I had him cowed, and he sat too, looking about as relaxed as a taxpayer undergoing an IRS audit. I gave his living room a quick once-over; it was small, bachelor-messy, and not nearly as well-furnished as Rojek's, to say nothing of the Polly Mars–Noreen James digs. At this rate, I'd be able to free-lance an article on the varied life-styles of New York singles for one of the shelter magazines.

"Okay, here's the story," I said, leaning forward. "Mr. Wolfe has a client—"

"Ha! Of course," Halliburton snapped. "That's it. Wolfe's trying to make money off all this, and—"

"Look," I said coldly, returning the interruption, "you don't much like having me here. Well, the more you butt in, the longer I'm going to stay. If I were you, I'd keep my mouth shut and my ears open." I had the same urge to belt him that I did the night he shot off his mouth in front of Morgana's, but I suppressed it. "As I started to say, Mr. Wolfe has a client, Noreen James, and—"

"Noreen?" His eyes widened and his eyebrows went up again. "*She's* the one who hired Wolfe?"

124 • ROBERT GOLDSBOROUGH

"Right," I said, ignoring the latest intrusion. "Does that surprise you?"

"Um, no, I guess not." He shrugged. "I mean, he is her brother and all."

"You obviously know Miss James."

Another shrug. "Well, I met her, when she was out with Sparky, you know."

"What was your impression of her?"

"How do you mean?"

"I thought the question was clear. What did you think of her?"

Halliburton still looked as if he were visiting the IRS. "A nice girl—really nice," he said woodenly.

"She seems to like you too," I ventured.

"Oh, yeah?" His face finally lost its sneer.

"So she told me. Did you ever go out with her?"

"Me? Hey, Sparky and I were good friends, you know? I wouldn't have a date with somebody he was interested in."

"How long had you and Linville known each other?"

"Oh, I guess maybe three, four years. I ran into him in one of the places one night, and we hit it off good. We were both just out of school."

"But not the same school?"

He dismissed the question with a wave of the hand. "Hell, no. Sparky went to a couple of those fancy little colleges up in New England. Me, I'm City U all the way."

"But you two palled around a lot?"

I could tell that Halliburton was running out of patience. "Hell, we hit the same spots, sometimes together. Sometimes we'd just run into each other."

"With the kind of money Linville had—and seemed to enjoy spending—wasn't it kind of expensive keeping up with him?" I asked.

"Hey, I got a little money of my own," he muttered. "Besides, Sparky, he enjoyed being, well, generous, you know?"

"Meaning he picked up the tab a lot?"

Halliburton grunted a yes.

"Ever go out on dates together?"

"Yeah, a few times, not very often."

"Been to his apartment?"

"Once or twice, but what of it? Listen, what do you want, anyway? Who do you and Wolfe think got Sparky if it wasn't James?"

"I'll just be another minute or two," I said, ignoring the question. "Why do you think Michael James—or anybody else, for that matter—would want to kill Linville?"

A shrug. "Hey, I've been asking myself that question for four days."

"Come on," I said, "you've got to have some idea about why James was so hot. And weren't you curious, at least a little bit, about why I wanted to talk to your friend on the street last Wednesday night in front of Morgana's?"

"Hey, with all the harassing Sparky had been getting from the press after that last speeding ticket, I just figured it was another reporter."

"But you told the police you recognized me."

It was air-conditioned in Halliburton's apartment, but perspiration droplets had formed on his forehead and his neck. "All right," he said defensively, "but still, I just figured you were out to hassle Sparky somehow because of his, well, his fast life, you know? He'd gotten to be kind of a target. People would recognize him on the street and give him a hard time, you know?"

"And you protected him by swearing at them. Courageous of you. Now, let's go through this together, and then I'll be gone from here, I promise. According to the newspapers, Michael James was looking for Linville the night he was killed, and he—James—made no bones about being angry with him, although even after he confessed, he apparently wouldn't say *why* he was so sore. What's your theory?"

Halliburton cursed under his breath, probably revving his brain cells trying to figure out how to get rid of me. "I don't have one, except that . . ."

"Go on," I said.

"Well, I suppose it must have had something to do with Noreen," he said tightly.

"Good thinking. But what?"

"How should I know? I wasn't in the habit of gabbing with Sparky about his social life."

"If you had to guess, what would make a brother angry—very angry—with someone who had spent time with his sister?"

Halliburton spread his hands. "Well, I mean, there's an obvious answer to that."

"Right. Which is?"

"Look, if you're trying to get me to say something bad about a friend, and one who's dead, for God's sake, forget it. They just buried the guy yesterday!"

"So are you saying you don't know anything about the extent of Linville's relationship with Noreen James, or you know but you're not talking?"

Halliburton swore. That boy had a very broad vocabulary. "I don't know squat," he said, his voice rising. "But it seems like everything you're telling me makes it look bad for the brother. Whatever happened between Sparky and Noreen, it sounds to me like the cops got the right guy. Now, is there anything else you want to talk about? If not, I got things to do."

"Two more questions," I said, standing as an enticement for him to answer. "As one of Linville's good friends, can you think of anyone else who might wish him ill?"

"Nobody," he answered, also getting up. "Sparky was a warm, fun-loving, good guy. He'd do anything for a friend."

I let the remark stand without comment. "Okay, last question: What happened after you two left Morgana's last Wednesday night?"

"How do you mean?"

"Where did you go? How long were you and Linville together?"

Halliburton pressed his lips together. "I've been over all this with the cops."

"Fine, now you can go over it with me."

I got a sigh and a roll of the eyes, but he knew he wasn't getting rid of me until he answered. "We took a cab to a little place several blocks farther along Second Avenue, the Owl, and had a couple of beers, then I left around eleven-thirty or so and took a cab home. Sparky had parked his car a few blocks away and he offered to drive me—but I said no thanks. That's way out of his way."

"So he stayed in the Owl?"

"Just to finish his drink. He said he wanted to make one or two more stops—maybe Orion, he said—and . . . that's the last I saw of him, sitting at the bar."

"Did you run into anybody you knew there?"

"Uh-uh." He shrugged. "It wasn't a place either of us went much. I think I'd only been in there one other time."

"All right," I said coolly. "I guess that'll hold me—at least for now." I walked into the foyer, with Halliburton trailing in my wake. I opened the door, pivoted toward him with a neutral expression, and went out into the hallway. Somebody in the building had had corned beef and cabbage for Sunday dinner. The door slammed behind me—hard—and his voice came through the wood clearly: "From now on, stay away from here," he said.

The big bully.

SEVENTEEN

Although it didn't seem that late, my watch insisted on telling me it was twenty past two when I got out of a cab in front of the brownstone. After my session with Todd Halliburton, I had toyed with walking north from the Village, which I've done on several occasions, but instead decided to use some of Noreen James's money. After all, I'd just had to spend fifteen minutes with a two-legged weasel, and it seemed to me that that act alone entitled me to something, say another taxi ride.

I buzzed to get in, which, given Fritz's absence, meant rousting Wolfe from the office to unlock the front door. He swung it open, scowling. "Well, did you miss me?" I asked cheerfully.

"Inspector Cramer telephoned twenty minutes ago," was his tart response. "The weapon presumably used to dispatch Mr. Linville has been located."

"You've got my attention," I said when we were in the office. "I'm all ears."

"That is comforting to know," Wolfe replied with no trace of irony. "It was indeed a tire iron," he said after getting himself resettled behind his desk, a feat roughly comparable to docking the *QE2*. "Apparently the one missing from that pile of tools on the floor in the parking garage. The inspector reported that it was found in a trashcan several doors east of where Mr. Linville lived by a building superintendent."

"And James said he went west from the garage."

Wolfe moved his head imperceptibly, which for him constitutes a nod. "Mr. Cramer has a dilemma. As you know, he has arrested someone who readily—almost eagerly—confessed to the murder of Barton Linville, relieving him and the police of intense media and civic pressure. But in so doing, he also took into custody a young man, the members of whose family he has known with affection for more than a generation."

"Nobody ever said life is easy, particularly for a public servant," I countered. I can be philosophical at times, despite what anybody says.

"Granted. However, I am inclined to extend a minimum of compassion to the inspector in this instance."

"That's doggone decent of you."

"Or practical," Wolfe remarked dryly. "When Mr. Cramer telephoned, I told him I wanted you to view the purported weapon."

"I'll bet that got a laugh."

"Hardly. He agreed without complaint."

"He *is* in a bind."

"Yes. He knows he has the wrong person but can do nothing about it and will climb into any lifeboat that will pull him aboard."

"Even one with Nero Wolfe manning the oars?" I asked.

"Yes. He said that you should call Sergeant Stebbins, who will arrange for you to see the tire iron at police headquarters."

So that was why, while Saul Panzer and his out-of-town visitor were using my tickets at Shea Stadium watching Dwight Gooden throw a two-hitter against St. Louis in a game that included a Mets' triple play, I was down at One Police Plaza visiting Purley Stebbins, who, like Cramer, seems never to take time off. A word here about the estimable sergeant: Purley is an old-school policeman, make no mistake. And he *looks* like an old-line cop ought to look, at least as I visualize it. He's big without being fat, probably only an inch taller than me but a lot thicker. You'd be pressing it to call Purley handsome, but he's got a strong face: big ears, big square jaw, bristly brows over eyes that don't miss a thing. He doesn't laugh much, but then, in his line of work, he doesn't see a whole lot to laugh about. He doesn't like criminals of any variety, and he isn't much fonder of private detectives, including me and Wolfe. Oh, he's usually civil, at least as civil as Purley ever gets, but he doesn't waste words and he doesn't conceal his disdain for anyone who makes money doing what he feels only the police are qualified to do. And besides, he thinks Wolfe has made him look bad a couple of times, which is hard to argue with.

But Purley also follows the chain of command scrupulously, and if Cramer tells him to bark, he barks—without complaint. "Okay, here we are," he gruffed after we had entered a small windowless, colorless room where a stocky little guy with glasses and a white smock was doing paperwork at a high table.

"Jenks, show us the item," Purley said tonelessly.

Jenks, who was wearing what looked like surgical gloves, opened a drawer in a gray cabinet and drew out a silver-colored L-shaped tire iron, the longer leg of which measured about a foot. "No touching," he cautioned like an elementary-school teacher as he held it out.

"Looks like dried blood," I said in my most professional voice, remarking on the brownish discoloration around the elbow of the tool.

"Could be," Jenks said.

"Yeah, could be," Purley echoed, throwing me a "You've-seen-it-and-I've-done-my-duty-so-now-go-home" expression. I had indeed seen all I wanted to, but Purley always brings out the worst in me, so I kept peering at the iron, which Jenks clasped tightly. "Find any prints?" I asked.

Jenks looked at Stebbins for some sign as to whether he should respond, and Purley, bless his uncomplicated self, shook his head. No subtlety there.

"Okay, that's enough, let's go," he told me. "Thank you, Mr. Jenks."

The little man nodded without expression as we walked out. In the hall, I thanked Purley for his hospitality and told him Wolfe also was appreciative, which must have impressed him, because he blinked once, or maybe it was twice.

Back at the brownstone after yet another taxi ride that would go onto Noreen James's bill, I rang the bell, and had the door unbolted and opened by Fritz, recently returned from wherever he spent the day—I didn't ask. In the office, I found Wolfe leaning back with his eyes closed.

"Taking a catnap?" I asked innocently as I slid into my chair.

He snorted, opening his eyes but making no other moves. "Report," he said.

"Do you mean on my trip downtown to look at the apparent murder weapon, or on all my activities of today?"

"Both," he said, ringing for beer.

With that, I reconstructed my visits to both Rojek and Halliburton, giving Wolfe plenty of the dialogue, which he appreciates, but making no value judgments. It took me twenty-three minutes.

"Your impressions of the two men?" he asked after I had finished.

"Mixed; I'll take them one at a time. First, Rojek: basically a decent guy, although more than a tad on the stuffy side. If he has a sense of humor, he's learned to suppress it masterfully. His feelings about Noreen James? Intense, and he's obviously interested in her for the long haul—he said as much without hesitation, and I believe him. Did he kill Linville? Possibly. My initial reaction is to say 'no way,' but then, he appears to be in love with her. And love, or so I've heard, can do strange things to a man's character, especially when the object of his affection has been ill-used. Take that crazy case over in Jersey where the meek little clothing-store stock clerk shot and wounded the professional wrestler who—"

"Enough!" Wolfe growled, holding up a palm and making a face. "You've made your point. What of Mr. Halliburton?"

"I don't have any higher opinion of him now than when I had the pleasure of meeting him in front of Morgana's. If he was less rude this time, it was mainly because we were one-on-one and he was scared stiff I'd pop him, which I admit was damned tempting. He's a little snake, and I get the impression that he hung around with Linville not so much out of friendship as because Linville had nice cars and good-looking women and spent money like water on himself and his friends."

"Would he have done his friend in?"

"Halliburton? I don't think so. He's not only a snake, he's a coward to boot."

"But your impression is that he was fond of Miss James?"

I nodded. "Very fond. And I guess the few times they met he must have cleaned up his act, because she seemed to think he was more or less bearable. But I don't see him conking anybody, let alone a friend, with a chunk of iron."

"The tire iron," Wolfe said. "You saw it?"

"In the presence of Purley Stebbins himself, no less. It is, well . . . a tire iron. Complete with what appears to be dried blood."

"Fingerprints?"

"Interesting you should ask. I posed that question to Stebbins and the guy who keeps watch over murder weapons and such, and they weren't in the mood to tell me."

Wolfe pressed his lips together once or twice. "Get Inspector Cramer," he said curtly.

I dialed and Stebbins answered on the second ring. When I told him Wolfe wanted to talk to his boss, he balked. "Look, he called Mr. Wolfe earlier today," I told him. "This is on the same matter." That drew some muffled grumbling at the other end, which sounded promising. I nodded to Wolfe to pick up.

"Yeah?" Cramer was his usual suave self.

"Inspector, as you know, Mr. Goodwin a short time ago viewed the tire iron that may have been used to kill Mr. Linville. He asked if fingerprints had been found on it and received no answer."

Cramer swore and covered his mouthpiece, but not well enough to drown out the chewing-out he gave Purley. The gist was "I told you to cooperate with Goodwin," although he used a number of additional adjectives that I have elected to omit from this narrative. "There were no prints found on the iron," Cramer said between deep breaths after he had finished his harangue. "Looks like the thing was wiped clean."

"What about the discoloration Mr. Goodwin observed?"

After a pause, Cramer responded. "Blood, Type O, same as Linville's. But, hell, damn near half the population is Type O."

"Thank you, sir," Wolfe told him. "I have a favor to request."

"Another one?" Cramer snapped.

"Yes. Has the weapon's discovery been made known to the press yet?"

"No. The damn thing only turned up this morning. The D.A.'s office doesn't even know about it yet. Why?"

"I would like to ask that, at least for twenty-four hours, news of the weapon be withheld, even from the district attorney's office."

"For God's sake, why?"

"Because such action, or more correctly lack of

action, may well be helpful in determining the identity of Mr. Linville's murderer," Wolfe said evenly.

"Balls!" Cramer roared. The only other sound that came through the wires for a quarter of a minute was his heavy breathing. "I'll think about it," he finally said, slamming his phone down. At that moment the doorbell rang, and I got up, beating Fritz to the hall. I took one peek through the one-way panel and did a quick about-face back to the office.

"We've got some interesting visitors on the stoop," I said to Wolfe, who had just returned to his book. "Megan and Doyle James, by name. Instructions?"

EIGHTEEN

Wolfe treated me to one of his high-grade scowls, the kind he reserves for occasions that upset his schedule. The scowl deepened as the doorbell chimed a second time. "All right," he grumped. "Show them in."

"This is a surprise." I smiled at the former husband and wife as I swung open the front door. "To what do we owe the honor?"

I got no smiles in return. "We're here to see Wolfe," said Megan, who was wearing a gray rough-silk number and an overdose of Opium. She looked grim as she stepped in ahead of Doyle, who had a pretty somber expression himself. "We know he almost never goes out, so don't try to tell us he's not here," she went on.

"I wouldn't dream of it," I replied lightly, still smiling as we moved along the hall toward the office. Wolfe glanced up from his book as we entered, and I made the introductions.

"Mr. Wolfe," Megan said before I had a chance to even seat them, "we're here to talk to you about your so-called investigation. We—"

"Madam, if you please," Wolfe said, "I prefer that those with whom I converse be at eye level. And since I have no intention of rising, it is in your best interests to be seated." That took some of her momentum away, which was of course the intent, and I

gestured her to one of the yellow chairs while Doyle
staked out the red-leather place of honor.

"Now, you wish to discuss what you choose to
term my 'so-called investigation'?" Wolfe asked blandly.

"Yes, we do. We—Doyle and I—want to know
precisely what's going on, and why we haven't heard
anything from you." Each word was loaded. "I think
we are owed an explanation."

"Indeed?" Wolfe's face registered the kind of surprise that sometimes makes me believe Hollywood lost
a great talent. "I'm not aware of any debt to you on
my part. You are not clients of mine."

"Our daughter is!" Megan hissed, and Doyle nodded slowly, leaning forward.

"And she is an adult," Wolfe said. "My compact is
with her and her alone, and, lacking her express
approval, I will discuss my progress with no one else."

"Well, have you been keeping her posted on that
so-called progress?" Doyle squared his shoulders and
folded his arms across his chest. "Isn't that part of
your compact?"

"Sir, I am not aware that your daughter is unhappy with my performance. If she is, she has not
chosen to inform me of this dissatisfaction. However,
your arrival, while unexpected, is not ill-timed. Had
you not come here, you would each have been paid a
visit by Mr. Goodwin."

"Oh? And why is that?" Doyle asked.

"Before we go on, will either of you have something to drink? My preference is for beer."

"Why not? I'll have a beer too," Doyle said, drawing a sharp look from his ex-wife. Wolfe reached
under his desk and hit the buzzer, signaling Fritz as to
how many beers he should bring in.

"Mr. Wolfe, we didn't come here to drink—or at
least I didn't—we came for answers." Megan was hot.
She also was craving a cigarette, but I could tell from
watching her that she'd searched the office for an

ashtray. There weren't any. "It's hardly necessary to remind you that our son's life is at stake."

"You are correct, madam—a reminder *is* superfluous. Now, let us get to specifics: Can you account for your time on the night of the twenty-sixth, last Wednesday?"

I enjoyed watching her trying to control her facial spasms. "What kind of a question is that?" she shrieked. "Are you going to try earning one of your preposterous fees by manufacturing suspects willynilly?"

Wolfe considered her dubiously. "Does the question pose a problem for you?"

"No, it does not," she said, spacing her words again. "I happened to be at home all evening. I was still unpacking from the trip to Europe."

"Were others there as well?"

"Michael stopped over for a few minutes just after dinner, to see how Noreen was. And you know, of course, that Noreen was—and is—staying with me. I wouldn't have her anywhere else after what I found out the night before." She glared at Doyle, as if accusing him of not keeping proper watch over their offspring during her extended sojourn in Europe.

"And you both were home all evening?" Wolfe asked.

"I was, although Noreen went out for a walk later—sometime near ten, I think. I tried to discourage her, given all that had happened, but she said she needed to get some air and do some thinking."

"So when she was gone, you were home alone?"

"That is correct," Megan said.

"Does your building have a doorman?"

"Of course."

"Then he will confirm that you did not go out?"

She sent Wolfe a look that would have wilted a cactus. "I don't see that my comings and goings are any concern whatever of yours."

"You can't have it both ways," Wolfe said, pour-

ing beer from one of the frosty bottles Fritz noise-
lessly brought in, two of which went to Wolfe, with the
third placed on the small table next to Doyle James,
along with a chilled pilsner glass. "You express concern that I am not adequately representing your daughter's interests in a matter that we concur is of overriding
importance to your son. Yet you bridle at my questions when I attempt to delve into this imbroglio."

"Well, what about it, Megan?" Doyle James said,
turning toward his ex-spouse. "Let's not pussyfoot
around, for God's sake. If you went out, you'd better
tell him about it, because it's going to come out sooner
or later."

"Oh, go to hell, Doyle. When I need your counsel, I'll ask for it, but don't hold your breath. I never
got any advice from you that was worth following in
the years we were together." Megan turned back to
Wolfe. "All right, dammit, I did go out, soon after
Noreen did. I felt boxed in by the place, big as it is. I
went to see a friend."

"Pamsett, of course," Doyle said, chuckling.

"Pamsett, of course," Megan mimicked him. "As
a matter of fact, that's exactly where I was: at Edward
Pamsett's apartment on Park in the Eighties. I needed
somebody to talk to. He's an old friend—you've met
him, Mr. Goodwin."

I nodded to show I was paying attention.

"How long were you there?" Wolfe asked.

"God, I don't know. I guess I went out around
ten or so; as I said, it was after Noreen had left on
her walk. It must have been . . . oh, twelve-thirty or
thereabouts when I got back home. I remember seeing
that Noreen's door was closed, so I knew she was
back."

"Although you didn't see her?"

"No—but when she's staying with me, she always
leaves the bedroom door open if she's going out."

"You took cabs to and from Mr. Pamsett's residence?"

"Yes, but I can't supply you with the drivers' names or numbers. Sorry," Megan said snidely.

Wolfe ignored the barb and turned toward Doyle. "Mr. James, can you account for your time Wednesday night?"

"I can tell you where I was," he said blandly, allowing himself a grin.

"Please do."

"I've got two places, a town house over in Jersey, near Princeton, and an apartment in Manhattan, because I enjoy coming into town."

"I'll just bet you do," Megan said archly. "Next I suppose you're going to tell us it's because of the great theater here."

Doyle gave her one of those smiles that isn't a smile and took a healthy swig of beer, from the bottle. "I apologize for my ex-wife's interruption," he said to Wolfe. "Anyway, I come into New York once or twice a week—and, yeah, sometimes it's to go to the theater. In fact, last Wednesday night I was here for just that reason—to see a show. Unfortunately, the lady I was going to take became ill at the last minute and I ended up giving the tickets away."

"So now we know what you *didn't* do that night," Wolfe remarked. He's a genius at deduction.

"Right. I ended up going out to dinner—alone—at a favorite spot of mine, a little French place on East Fifty-third. The maître d' can vouch for me—I'm sure he's still got his reservation list from that night, and I'll be happy to give you his name."

"When did you leave the restaurant?"

"As we've been talking, I've been trying to estimate the time. I'd say around ten," Doyle said. "It was a nice night, so I walked across town to my place, which is over near the UN Building. I probably got there around, oh, ten-thirty, ten-forty, something like that. I know it was before eleven, because I caught the eleven-o'clock news on TV."

"Can anyone vouch for the time of your arrival at home?"

"I really doubt it," Doyle said. "My building has a doorman, but he doesn't keep track of comings and goings. His nose is usually buried in some book."

"We came here to get answers, and all we've been doing is giving them, which I find to be both insulting and degrading," Megan pronounced nasally. "Now, tell us what's going on. We've got a right to know."

Wolfe considered her and frowned. "Madam, we have already been over this ground, and to retrace our steps would be fruitless. Good afternoon." He got to his feet, walked around the desk, and marched into the hall, turning toward the kitchen.

"The arrogance!" Megan said, turning in her chair to watch his departure. "The man doesn't have a shred of common courtesy."

"I don't seem to recall your making an appointment to see Mr. Wolfe," I said. "What would Miss Manners have said about people who drop in unannounced?"

"Hah!" Doyle James said, slapping his knee. "You've got yourself a point there, Goodwin. I told Megan we probably wouldn't accomplish a thing by coming here, but she insisted. She thinks she can get anyplace with anybody by bullying them."

"But you tagged along anyway, I notice," Megan snapped.

"Hell, if only to save you from yourself, my dear," he replied with an impish grin. "Somebody has to tell you when it's time to go. And it's time. Say good night, Gracie."

Megan James was so livid she was speechless, which was a relief. They both got up, and I rose with them, following them out. Not a word was spoken as we walked down the hall, but after I swung the door open and Megan stalked out, Doyle gave me a wink.

It was nice to see he was in such apparently good spirits, because he'd need them. If those two were

THE LAST COINCIDENCE • 141

planning to share a taxi, even for a few blocks, he would need all the humor he could generate to keep from getting roasted by his former mate. Something about his good spirits was troubling, though. After all, wasn't this a man whose daughter had been attacked and his son arrested for murder? Was I off base, or shouldn't he be *angrier* than he appeared to be? I resolved to think about that.

NINETEEN

After bolting the door behind the battling Jameses, I went to the kitchen, where I found Wolfe and Fritz staring glumly into a pot on the counter.

"Don't tell me it's another one of your arguments over what should go into the perfect New Orleans bouillabaisse," I said in mock disgust. "The Israelis and the Arabs will be going to block parties together before the two of you agree on this one. Making any progress?"

That got no reaction whatever. Wolfe muttered to Fritz and Fritz muttered back. And more things, I didn't pay attention to what they were, got tossed into the bouillabaisse, but neither of them acknowledged my presence. I was feeling neglected.

"Will you be needing my services any more today?" I finally asked Wolfe.

He looked up as if I had shrieked during a séance. "I will not," he said absently, turning his attention back to the pot.

"Okay, good luck with your soup," I said, walking out and feeling two glares aimed at my back. The remark was directed to both of them, and to be honest, it was made with malice aforethought. Referring to bouillabaisse as soup is like calling someone's Lhasa apso a pooch.

I went to my desk in the office and dialed Lily's number, getting her after two rings. "My day so far has been fraught with difficulties," I told her, "but suddenly there appears to be a break in the storm, if you'll allow a literary allusion, and I thought perhaps we might take this opportunity to dine together and share our dreams and aspirations."

"Ever the sweet-talker," she said. "And although I could take umbrage at being asked so late, I will overlook that egregious breach of etiquette and accept, conditionally, of course."

"Egregious, eh? You're getting to sound more like Wolfe all the time. Okay, state the condition."

"That we dine at Rusterman's, of course. I'm saving La Ronde for my birthday."

"Sold. I'll be by to get you in a taxi, honey—in twenty minutes."

"For a second there, I thought you were onto a really catchy lyric," she said. "But somehow, the 'in-twenty-minutes' part needs work."

"If you like it, I'll tinker with it," I replied. "Better not be late."

"I think you're onto something, fella," she said, hanging up.

A half-hour later, Lily and I were in our favorite corner booth in the small upstairs room at Rusterman's, courtesy of Franz, the current owner.

"Well, Escamillo," she said after we'd ordered a drink and I'd given her a quick summary of the visit to the brownstone by Megan and Doyle, "now how do you like dealing with various members of my family?"

"Mixed, if I have to reduce it to a single word."

"Care to get more specific, or has Nero Wolfe sworn you to secrecy?"

I lifted one eyebrow, grinning. "With you, I'm always happy to get specific. I'll blab all you want, but there's a price."

"Naturally there is—and knowing you, it's answers to some questions."

"M'God, you are perceptive," I replied, proceeding to tell her, in varying degrees of detail, what had transpired over the last couple of days.

"Interesting," she said as we attacked our salads. "Sounds like our Megan is running true to form."

"So is Wolfe. I'm worried that after today's session with her, he may suffer a complete relapse and withdraw to his plant rooms and his food and his books and his beer forever, poor chap."

"Nonsense. Megan isn't worth the grief, although the way you've just painted the situation, it doesn't sound like grief—it sounds exactly like the way your boss lives now."

"Okay, so maybe I exaggerated a bit. Now for a question: Is your sister—make that half-sister—capable of murder? And if the answer is yes, would she let her own son take the fall for it?"

"That's really two questions, but you know that I'm a good sport. Answer to the first part—yes, assuredly. I think Megan would kill if, one, it suited her purposes and, two, if she thought she could get away with it. As to the second part—that's a lot tougher. She and Michael haven't gotten along, to say the least. I told you that there is some uncertainty as to his father's identity. Several years ago, during either his freshman or sophomore year in college, Michael found out—I've never known how—that there was a question about his parentage.

"The upshot is that rather than being mad at the man purported to be his father, a guy—I met him once and was unimpressed—who now lives in Europe, he took it out on Megan, suggesting in somewhat graphic terms that she was, shall we say, a woman of less-than-exemplary morals. His conservative nature—and God, is he conservative, especially for someone his age—drove him to outrage over what his mother had done. They were very close before that, but they haven't been since, although they do maintain a civility toward each other. Anyway, despite the rancor, I'd have to say that I don't believe Megan would let him take the fall, to use your term."

"So you're giving her a pass?" I asked as we each started in on our roast leg of lamb.

"You asked me a question, Escamillo—make that two questions—and I tried to answer them honestly, based on my knowledge of my half-sister's behavior and temperament. If that's giving her a pass, then I'm guilty as charged, your honor."

"Time off for good behavior, case closed," I said between bites. "What about Doyle James? How do you rate him as a suspect? Based on your knowledge of his behavior and temperament, of course?"

"Archie, I'm sorry, but I have just as hard a time there. Like with Megan, I can see Doyle killing Linville, given the circumstances—in fact, it's a lot easier to picture him doing it than Megan. But where it falls apart for me again is that I can't conceive of him standing by and watching Michael go to prison, or whatever, for what he did."

"Even though he, Doyle, might not be Michael's father?"

"I don't think that matters—not to Doyle. I know he's had a pretty wild life, a lot of women, some hard drinking, some heavy spending. But almost all of that came after he and Megan got divorced, and he's essentially a very decent, honorable man. Rough around the edges, yes, and impulsive, but good-hearted and honest. If that's my heart talking rather than my head, dammit, so be it."

"I don't know him like you do—in fact I hadn't seen him for years until last week, and then again today. But I'd have to agree that he comes across as a stand-up kind of guy. And he knows how to zing Megan, which has to count for something somewhere."

"I sense my sister hasn't captivated you."

"Bingo. Speaking of your sister, whom we apparently can't avoid, what's your analysis of her well-tailored friend Pamsett, beyond what you told me the other day?"

"What you're really asking me is: Could Edward have done Linville in? I'd have to plead ignorance on that one. As I told you, I really don't know Edward very well, but I have a hard time picturing him picking up a tire iron in some dark, greasy garage. He'd get his hands dirty, to say nothing of the possibility of soiling his four-hundred-dollar sport coat."

"He does seem pretty far removed from grease and violence," I admitted.

"And besides," Lily said, "what would his motive be?"

"He doesn't seem the type, but might he have been playing hero for Megan by avenging her for what was done to her daughter?"

"How could he play hero if she didn't know about it? I mean, killers don't usually go around bragging, even to their lady-friends. And even in the unlikely event that (a) Edward Pamsett *did* kill Linville, and (b) Megan knew about it, she would hardly sacrifice her son to protect Pamsett. That much I can say for my sister."

"Point taken. While we're on the subject, how would you describe Megan's relationship with Pamsett?"

Lily took a sip of Zinfandel and dabbed her lips with her napkin. "Good question. It's possible that passion exists there that I'm not picking up on, but I really doubt it, knowing her and observing him. I think it's a case of each of them having someone to go to society functions with. They both eat up that type of thing—benefits, black-tie stuff, you know."

"Sure. Just the kinds of things you're always trying to get me to."

"Right, and Megan has a damn sight more success with Edward than I have with you."

"What do you mean? Just last month we went to that costume nonsense at the Churchill."

"Right. And remember how you whined about it?"

"That's just because I didn't like the idea of dressing as Henry the Eighth. Anyway, you think Megan and Pamsett are platonic pals who mainly provide each other with half of a couple so that dinner parties they go to come out with even numbers?"

"Seems reasonable. Plus the fact that they genuinely get along. Edward is laid-back and easygoing, as you probably could tell, being, by your own admission, a shrewd judge of character. He's one of those rare people who can put up with Megan and her irascibility, and do so cheerfully. Also, he's a decent-looking escort, what with that wavy salt-and-pepper Hollywood hair and all. Kind of a cross between Douglas Fairbanks, Jr. and Ronald Colman, and every bit as debonair as both of them."

"I wish somebody would describe *me* that way sometime."

"Oh, stop with that. I've already told you that you've got *savoir vivre*. Isn't that enough to salve your insecurities?"

"I'll try to let it comfort me," I sniffed. "Megan told Wolfe that on the night Linville was killed, she spent a couple of hours at Pamsett's place, just talking."

"Actually, I don't doubt that," Lily said. "She's told me a couple of times that one of the things she likes most about Edward is that he's a wonderful listener. She was probably over there talking the poor sap's leg off."

"That gives her an alibi at least for the earlier portion of the evening."

"Which, from the tone of your voice, doesn't exactly please you."

"Oh, maybe so, but the time after midnight is still at least partly unaccounted for. Let me pose an academic question: If—and I'm only saying if—Megan wasn't at Pamsett's abode at all on Wednesday night, would he lie for her and say that she was?"

Lily looked down at her nearly clean plate and wrinkled the loveliest forehead on the eastern seaboard. She thought for several heartbeats before looking up. "Interesting academic question. You like to express opinions in odds," she said, "so I'll speak your language. I'd say it's two-to-one that, yes, he'd lie for her if she asked him to. But if I may be allowed to anticipate your next question, I'd also give you five-to-two that she didn't ask him to tell a story for her because she *was* at his place when she says she was."

"You're quite an anticipator," I told her. "Or is there such a word?"

"Probably, but on that, I'll yield to your boss—words are his department. Now I'll anticipate your next move: Be it tonight or tomorrow, you are going to pay a visit to Mr. Pamsett."

"I've become totally transparent!" I said. "The woman can read my mind."

"It took you long enough to figure that out. Why do you think I'm always one step ahead of you—except of course when I don't want to be?"

"I've always wondered," I admitted. "Do you want to be one step ahead of me now?"

My answer was a wink and a smile. I returned the smile and we ordered dessert.

TWENTY

It was almost eleven when I climbed out of a cab in front of the brownstone. I rang the bell, knowing the bolt would be on at that hour, and within seconds Fritz pulled open the door. "Archie, there is a man waiting for you in the front room," he said in a whisper as I entered the hall. "He has been in there for more than two hours. He wanted to see Mr. Wolfe, but he was up in the plant rooms when the gentleman came and he didn't want to be disturbed. When I told Mr. Wolfe his name, he told me to let him in and have him wait for you."

"Why don't you tell *me* his name?" I asked impatiently. "And stop whispering; you know as well as I do that the front-room door is soundproofed."

Fritz colored, as he does when I chide him about anything. "He is Edward Pamsett. Very much the gentleman, very nicely dressed. I have looked in on him many times, to see if he would like to keep on waiting, and he always says yes. He is reading magazines in there. He doesn't even want coffee or anything else to drink. I have made the offer three times."

"Where's Mr. Wolfe?"

"Up in his bedroom. He was in the office reading until about ten minutes ago. I told him when he went upstairs that Mr. Pamsett was still here, and he told me to allow him to remain for thirty more minutes, and then, if you hadn't returned, to request that he leave."

"All right. I'll see him now. Thanks." Fritz nodded and went off to the kitchen, where I knew he would remain as long as we had a visitor in the house. He hates the idea that a guest might request food and not be able to get it, or worse yet, might have to rely on me to rustle something up. Fritz does not place great faith in my culinary abilities.

"Good evening," I said, opening the door to the front room.

"Oh . . . yes . . . Mr. Goodwin," Edward Pamsett said, dropping the magazines and springing to his feet. "Do you remember me? We met at Megan James's last week."

"Of course I do, Mr. Pamsett," I said, admiring his summer-weight double-breasted blue blazer with color-coordinated silk challis tie and dark blue handkerchief cascading out of his breast pocket. "I understand you've been waiting for some time."

"I . . . yes, yes. I apologize for not calling for an appointment. I should have, of course, but . . . well, although you may not believe this, sometimes I'm rather impulsive."

"I'll take your word for it. Why don't we go into the office to talk?" I opened the connecting door, steering him through and over to the red leather chair. "Now, what brings you here on a Sunday night?" I asked brightly, sliding into my desk chair and pivoting to face him.

"I had come to talk to Mr. Wolfe—or you, of course—I understand you report everything to him more or less verbatim?"

"Not more or less."

"Uh . . . yes, verbatim. Anyway, Megan called me today—about . . . last Wednesday night." Pamsett fiddled with the dimpled knot of his tie and glanced around the office, expecting me to respond. Not wanting to be predictable, I remained silent, watching him fidget.

"Anyway," he said, making a production out of

THE LAST COINCIDENCE • 151

clearing his throat, "she told me that she and Doyle
had been here earlier today and that she mentioned
her visit to see me Wednesday night."

"Correct."

"Yes, well, the reason I'm here, basically, is to
corroborate that she was with me from . . . as nearly
as I can recall, a little after ten until about right around
midnight. You understand, those are approximate
times, but I think they're pretty close. When she left, I
went down with her to the lobby of my building to
make sure she was safely in a taxi." He smiled self-
effacingly and turned his palms up, as if indicating
there was nothing more to be said on the matter.

"Mr. Pamsett, one thing puzzles me: You could
have told me this over the phone in seconds; why
come all the way across town and wait for—what?
—two hours without an appointment or any guarantee that Mr. Wolfe or I would even be here?"

I got another one of Pamsett's humble smiles and
more of the palms-up business. "That's an appropri-
ate question, Mr. Goodwin. I can only say in my
defense that I invariably prefer face-to-face contact to
the telephone. But there's more to it than that."

"I felt sure that there was," I told him.

"Yes, well, Megan was unsettled by today's meeting with Mr. Wolfe, to say the least. I think she felt
her call on me on Wednesday night needed, as I said
before, some sort of corroboration. From my perspective, the situation was important enough to warrant
this visit."

"Did Mrs. James ask you to come here?"

"Actually, no," Pamsett said. This time the smile
was sheepish. "And I'd appreciate it if you didn't tell
her about this visit. She might view it as meddling,
although it surely isn't meant as such."

"All right, you've made the visit, and your corroboration is duly noted. Is there anything else?"

"Well . . . I guess not. I thought perhaps you
would have some questions."

"Questions? Let me see . . . All right, one thing you might be able to clarify: Did Mrs. James call you before she came to see you Wednesday night?"

Pamsett leaned back and folded his arms across his chest, looking up and making a production out of recollecting. "I . . . Yes, yes, she did," he said slowly. "Megan called me earlier in the evening and asked if she could come by."

"Is that a common occurrence?"

"I beg your pardon?"

"Is Mrs. James's calling you to ask if she can stop by a common occurrence?"

"No," he said stiffly, looking as if he was straining to keep a smile on his face.

"What did she say when she called you?"

"Just that she needed to talk. We spend a lot of time talking."

"About what?"

An elegant shrug. "All manner of things: her children, my children, politics, charitable organizations, the theater—all manner of topics."

"And what did she want to talk about Wednesday night?"

"Mr. Goodwin, is this confidential?" Pamsett said in a low voice, leaning forward and fixing me with a look that was meant to communicate that we were men of the world discussing elemental problems.

"Not necessarily," I replied. "I am a private investigator, licensed by the State of New York. If I learn that a crime has been committed, I am by law required to report what I know to the proper authorities. Beyond that, I honor the confidences of clients. As far as nonclients are concerned, however, I operate on a case-by-case basis."

"Understood," he said tightly, realizing that his "we're-both-men-of-the-world" approach wasn't working on me. "All right. I am going to elect to trust you."

"That's your choice, of course."

"Of course. When Megan came to my apartment Wednesday night, it was to talk about Noreen and . . . what had happened to her. She was concerned that, and I know this sounds ridiculous, that she might be viewed by Wolfe as a suspect in Linville's killing."

"I don't mean to sound either disrespectful or cynical, Mr. Pamsett, but how did Mrs. James think you could be of help in this area?"

"I think it was mainly that I have a sympathetic ear," he answered. "She knows that she can talk candidly to me without being judged or criticized."

"How would you describe your relationship with Mrs. James?"

"How do you mean?" What was left of his smile had evaporated.

"I thought the question was clearly stated. Answer it in whatever way seems natural. If I have a problem with your response, I'll say so."

"I find that a somewhat intrusive posture," Pamsett said, still trying to sound chummy, but with irritation showing around the edges.

"Suit yourself," I told him, "but remember, you're the one who urged me to ask you questions, and that was only a few minutes ago. Okay, now I'm asking. You can answer or not, that's your draw."

Pamsett crossed one leg over the other and contemplated the back of his hand. "Megan and I have known each other for . . . six, maybe seven years now. I am a widower, my children grown and gone to live in other parts of the country—and the world. Megan is of course divorced. We spend a good deal of time together. We eat out, go to concerts, shows, various civic and benefit functions. Quite simply, we have a lot in common and enjoy each other's company. If I may venture a comment—and not a disrespectful one, I assure you—I suspect our *relationship*, to use your term, is not wholly unlike the one you have with Megan's very charming and attractive half-sister."

He had me there. In fact, as he had been describing what the two of them do together, I was struck by the similarity to so many of my activities with Lily. "Point taken," I said, grinning to show that there were no hard feelings on my part. "Care to speculate on who might have bumped off Linville?"

Pamsett tugged on his ear, then shook his head. "I simply cannot believe it was Michael. The act is totally out of character for him, even given the enormity of the act committed by the Linville boy. But I certainly can think of no one else to nominate. Might I inquire as to what progress you and Mr. Wolfe are making in this direction?"

"Mr. Wolfe pretty much keeps his own counsel in these matters. For all I know, he may already have things figured out, but if that's the case, he hasn't chosen to share his thoughts with me."

Pamsett frowned, running a hand along the wavy gray-white hair on the side of his head. The guy really did look—and act—like something out of an English movie. "Do you have any idea at all when, or if, he is likely to make a determination?"

"Look, I'm sorry to be so vague, but one, you're not our client, and two, I'm not kidding when I say that Mr. Wolfe is pretty damn tight-lipped regarding his thought processes. I'm not even going to speculate on when he will choose to say something, let alone on *what* he will have to say."

"I see. All right, you've been most generous with your time, especially at this late hour," Pamsett said, making a move to get up.

"Oh, before you go, I have a question," I said casually.

"Yes."

"I wonder how you happened to be at the funeral services for Sparky Linville. And also at the cemetery."

Now, Pamsett is smooth, but not that smooth. The questions clearly got to him. At that, the guy handled himself pretty well. "Oh, yes, yes, I *was* at both. Nice services, don't you think? As to why I was there, that is a valid question," he conceded, nodding.

"I thought it was."

"Well, this is a little embarrassing, but only if the reason for my being there gets back to Megan."

"That seems unlikely."

"I'm glad to hear you say that. Well, in all candor, Mr. Goodwin, I went to the services because I was . . . well, afraid Megan would appear there and make some sort of scene—you know, berate the dead boy's parents and all."

"Doesn't that seem a little farfetched?"

"You don't know Megan very well," he replied earnestly.

"Perhaps not. But what would she gain from something like that?"

"Nothing, it's true. But I've watched Megan grow increasingly irrational over the last several months. And now, this horrible business with Noreen has just about put her over the brink."

"Are you suggesting Alzheimer's?"

"Oh, no, no. But she's definitely unbalanced. I have very great affection for Megan, Mr. Goodwin. I know a wonderful side of her—a side she allows far too few people to see. But she also has her demons, God help her." He gestured toward the ceiling.

"But couldn't you have just stayed with her the morning of the funeral? That would have prevented her from going."

"She would have seen right through that," Pamsett said, spreading his hands. "As it turned out, though, my precautions *were* unnecessary, weren't they? She wasn't there, and nothing happened."

"Nothing happened," I agreed.

"Well, I really must be going now. Thank you so much for your time," Pamsett said. I followed him down the hall to the door, suggesting that his best chance to get a cab quickly was at Eighth Avenue. He

thanked me and we shook hands like gentlemen before he stepped out into the night. David Niven was
never more elegant.

I thanked him too, albeit silently, for saving me a
trip to see him tomorrow.

TWENTY-ONE

On Monday morning, having had my more-or-less-standard breakfast of wheatcakes, sausage, eggs, juice, milk, and coffee, I was in the office a few minutes before nine bringing the orchid records up-to-date on the computer when the phone rang.

"Archie, I admit I'm slow, dammit, and it was only this morning that I made the connection, but the least you could have done was keep an old friend current on what was happening," Lon Cohen fired off after I'd said hello.

"Hey, explain yourself, old-timer," I answered.

"With pleasure. I was going back over our Sunday profile on Michael James, and it finally dawned on me that the Rowan who was his grandfather is the late father of a certain special friend of a certain licensed New York private investigator. That, coupled with your call to me the other day asking about Sparky Linville's murder, made me realize that something's probably going on that I should be looking into."

"Could be."

"Could be? What the hell kind of answer is that? Come on, Archie, how many times have you tapped me for information about cases you and Wolfe are working on?"

"And how many times have you and the *Gazette* gotten scoops on cases my eminent employer has blown the lid off, to slip in a phrase that we tough-talking detectives are supposed to use?"

"Okay, I concede that we've probably scratched each other's backs more or less equally over time. But today is today, and there are deadlines to be met. Is Wolfe trying to find somebody other than Michael James to stick with the Linville murder?"

"That's an interesting conjecture."

Lon lowered his voice and spoke slowly, enunciating each word. "Archie, there will be times again—and you know it—when you are going to need me." The boy's nothing if not subtle.

"You're right," I responded. "I think you might for this afternoon's edition like to suggest that unnamed sources have reported that Nero Wolfe has been looking into the case."

"God, is that the best you can do?"

"Right now it is, although I promise you that if and when anything happens, you'll be the first to know. You always have been in the past. Hell, a murder weapon hasn't even been found yet, has it?"

"Not as far as we know, but the James kid *has* confessed. What makes Wolfe think he isn't guilty?"

"Uh-uh. Nice try, friend, but for now you've got all I can give you."

"You don't make it any easier for me to do my job, Archie," Lon said reproachfully, and I countered that I wasn't aware I was on the *Gazette* payroll. With that, he used a word that Cramer also likes and hung up.

The doorbell rang as I cradled the phone. I walked down the hall, wondering what Cramer could possibly want this time, and was surprised to see our client through the one-way glass. "Come in," I said brightly. "I must confess I wasn't expecting you."

Her face looked as if she'd either been crying or been up all night, or maybe both. "I . . . had to see you," she said unevenly.

"Okay," I told her when she'd sunk into the red leather chair and I was at my desk, "you have my undivided attention."

"I killed him," Noreen pronounced coldly. "It was me."

"*You* killed Linville?"

"That's right." She was staring more or less in my direction, but without eye contact.

"Have you told the police?"

"No, I . . . thought you should know first. I feel terrible about . . . lying to you and Mr. Wolfe and all."

"And you were going to let your brother take the fall?" I asked sharply.

"No-o-o, I wouldn't have," she said, the tears starting. "At first I thought he'd retract his confession, but *he hasn't*. This is terrible!"

"It certainly is. All right, Noreen—how did you kill Linville?"

"You already know," she wailed. "In that garage—with a metal thing, you know."

"Tire iron?" I asked.

She nodded.

"How did you know where he kept his car?" I asked.

"I . . . He mentioned it one of the times we were out—he loved to talk about that car, he told me everything about it."

"You've got a good memory. Did you have to wait a long time for him to come home that night?"

"More than two hours."

"Did you wait inside the garage or in the street?"

"What difference does it make?" Noreen wailed.

"The police will want to know," I told her. "They like their facts all neat and tidy. How many times did you hit him? Did he bleed a lot?"

"God, I don't know, I don't know!" She was so loud now that Fritz popped his head in to see if anyone was being throttled. I waved him away.

"Did he say anything as he was falling?" I pushed on, but I didn't have to go any further. She had her head in her hands, racked with sobs. I handed her a handkerchief.

"Listen, Noreen," I told her after the waterworks had subsided, "I'm not even going to give you a 'Nice try' for that ludicrous performance. Mr. Wolfe is having enough trouble without having to deal with such a stunt. If I were to repeat your story to him, he'd throw me out on my ear, and I wouldn't blame him—to say nothing of what he'd do to you. I guess I can excuse this because you were doing it to save your brother, right?"

She nodded, still wiping an already badly smeared face. "You weren't very nice, though."

"If you'd gone to the police with that fairy tale, you'd have really gotten a taste of 'not very nice.' Now, Mr. Wolfe is going to be walking in here in less than ten minutes, and I think you'll agree it's a good idea if you're gone then. That is, if you still want to be a client."

Noreen nodded again, and I allowed her two minutes to whip out her compact and repair her face. She was so chagrined she didn't say another word, and I managed to hustle her out the front door at ten-fifty-seven.

Four minutes later, the groaning of the elevator told me Wolfe was descending from his two-hour séance with the orchids.

I got the usual morning greeting from him as he detoured around the corner of the desk, placed a raceme of *Oncidium schilleriana* in the vase on the blotter, and lowered himself into his favorite chair. "Before you start in on the mail, most of which is junk or just a cut above it, I have a report and a question," I said.

He gave me his standard raised-eyebrows look, and I went on. "First off, our client just left here. She dropped by to tell me she had killed Linville."

"Twaddle," Wolfe snorted, ringing for beer.

"Of course it's twaddle. I gave her a short—and

mild—sample of police interrogation and sent her packing."

"A sophomoric attempt to shield a sibling. I would have expected better from her," Wolfe said peevishly.

"Agreed. Anyway, on to the question. I'm curious as to why you didn't deign to meet with Mr. Pamsett when he stopped in last night. The poor lug spent two hours in the front room with our wonderful selection of magazines before I got home and talked to him."

"He had no appointment," Wolfe sniffed, starting in on the mail.

"Right, but we *are* working on a case, or so I've been led to believe. Now, I admit I'm a pretty damn good interrogator, but I also concede that you, being, as we all know, a genius, will often unearth information or form observations that elude me. Such might have been the case had you made the effort to see Mr. Pamsett."

Wolfe looked up from his mail with an expression that conveyed irritation. "Since I did not, I will be forced to rely upon your admittedly limited skills. Report."

I gave him a verbatim of our conversation, during which he kept his eyes closed. "Do you believe Mrs. James was with him in his apartment, as they both have stated?" Wolfe asked when I finished.

"I do. Her I could suspect of lying, but probably not Pamsett. He strikes me as the type who's a lousy liar—old school tie and all that. I'd give seven-to-two he's telling it straight. But say they *were* together until even midnight. What does that prove? Either of them could have easily gotten over to Linville's garage on East Seventy-seventh Street in time to use that tire iron on him. As you recall from Cramer and all the newspaper stories, he was killed after midnight."

"How would either of them know where he kept his car?" Wolfe posed.

I shrugged. "Even Michael James presumably

didn't know. By his own admission, if one chooses to believe it, he was hanging around outside the apartment and just happened to see Linville pulling into the garage. After all, it's only a few doors from his building. But if that's a feasible explanation for Michael James, it also becomes feasible for Pamsett or Megan."

"Among others," Wolfe said.

"Yeah, interesting, isn't it? On the night Linville cashes in, Doyle James, who lives much of the time over in Jersey, just happens to be in New York. And to add whipped cream to the sundae, this man-about-town has no alibi for that night, at least not for the time of death. Where's Noreen? Out walking till after twelve, no witnesses. Where's Polly Mars? At home, alone, no witnesses. Where's Rojek? At home, alone, no witnesses. Even that stooge Halliburton says he was home alone by that time. In fact, if I hadn't gotten home by a quarter past twelve and been let in by Fritz, even *I* wouldn't have an alibi. And then . . ."

I stopped talking because Wolfe couldn't hear me. He was leaning back with his eyes closed and his lips pushing out and in, out and in. When he's like that, there's no reaching him. Even he can't explain what happens to him during these times. But I'm convinced that if Fritz were to carry in a steaming plate of grilled starlings, which may well be his favorite dish, and wave it under his nose at a time like this, Wolfe wouldn't awaken. As I always do during these occurrences, I sat silently at my desk and timed the lip exercise. Fourteen minutes had passed when Wolfe blinked awake and sat up straight.

"Archie, does our car have a tire iron?"

"Sure, they all do, of one kind or another."

"What does ours look like?"

"Beats me. I've never had to use it."

"Get it, and bring it to me. Now."

"Okay," I said, wondering if this time Wolfe's cylinders had misfired during his trance. I got up, left the office as Wolfe was ringing for beer, and went out the front door, heading for the garage on Tenth Avenue between Thirty-fifth and Thirty-sixth where we've always kept our cars. At the garage, I said "Hi" to Bill Curran, who runs the place, and told him I wanted something from the Mercedes.

"Sure, Arch, it's in the usual spot," he said, going back to waxing his own car, a green Jaguar that he babies as if it were his only child, although I know for a fact he has three kids at home. Our Mercedes was indeed in its usual spot, toward the back of the garage on the street level, between a Bentley and another Jaguar. I opened the trunk with my key and found the fabric pouch of tools, which looked as if it had never been touched. I checked to make sure there was a tire iron inside and took the whole pouch with me, waving again to Bill as I left.

Back in the office, Wolfe was well along on his first bottle of beer of the day. "Here's the tool kit," I told him, knowing he wouldn't recognize one if it fell on him. "And here's the tire iron." I pulled it out and handed it across the desk. "By the way, I talked to Lon this morning, and he has heard nothing about the finding of a murder weapon, so Cramer apparently has kept it under wraps."

Wolfe took the iron in both hands, turning it and scrutinizing it. "Is this similar to the one Mr. Stebbins showed you?"

"Looks identical," I said. "L-shaped, and the same length."

"Satisfactory," Wolfe said. "Call Miss James and inform her that I have completed my investigation. Tell her I would like her to be here tonight, at nine o'clock. Also, I want Michael, Doyle, and Megan James present, as well as Mr. Pamsett, Mr. Rojek, and Miss Mars. And Miss Rowan too."

"As you ordain," I said. "Care to fill your faithful lapdog in on what this is all about?"

"After the calls have been made," Wolfe said,

sliding the tire iron into a desk drawer and picking up his book.

I got all of them, and they agreed to come, but not without a struggle. Noreen was easy, though; she was excited that something apparently had gotten resolved, and although she tried to ask me questions, I could tell her—honestly, this time—that I was as much in the dark as she. While I had her on the line, she asked, or maybe told, both her mother and her brother to come along. I could hear muffled grumbling in the background from a voice that sounded like Megan's, and then the Dragon Lady herself was on the line. "What is all this about a meeting?" she shrilled. "Haven't we indulged you and Wolfe enough?" I told her, in my most diplomatic tone, that it wasn't a matter of indulging me or Wolfe, but of acceding to her own daughter's wishes, which seemed to take most of the wind out of her sails. I got Lily next, and she was full of questions, but I deflected them and she said she'd of course make it.

It took me several calls and messages and callbacks to get the others, and it was after lunch when I finished. I reached Rojek at his Wall Street office; he grumbled but said he'd come when I said Noreen wanted him there. I had to get Polly Mars through her answering service. When she called back, she insisted that she had a night assignment, which I told her to drop. She did, not without some grousing about permanently lost income. Pamsett claimed a previous engagement too, but I pressed him, saying everybody else would be present, and he gave in. Doyle James was the hardest to locate, but by mid-afternoon he had checked in and said we could count on him.

At two-thirty-three I turned to Wolfe. "Okay, they'll all be here. Now what?"

"Get Mr. Cramer on the line."

I had expected that order, of course. As often happens when I call Cramer, the flunky who answered the phone wasn't cooperative and started grill-ing me about what Wolfe wanted. "I think the inspector will want to take this call," I said curtly. "Mr. Wolfe has information on a pending case."

"You can give it to me," the flunky said.

"Good-bye, pal," I told him, as both Wolfe and I cradled our receivers. "I've got a sawbuck says Cramer'll call in less than ten minutes," I said to Wolfe, whose face was set in a scowl.

"That was the correct handling of the situation," he said grudgingly. "I won't take the wager."

Three minutes and seventeen seconds later, the phone rang, and we lifted our instruments simulta-neously. "Wolfe!" Cramer bellowed. "What's going on?"

"Sir, you need to instruct your servitors as to the proper telephone etiquette," Wolfe replied.

"That's not why you called."

"Correct. My client, Miss James, will be here to-night at nine o'clock, as will her mother, father, and brother, in addition to three other persons: Edward Pamsett, Douglas Rojek, and Polly Mars. I will be making a significant announcement concerning Bar-ton Linville's death, and you also might wish to be present."

"Wolfe, given the circumstances, to say nothing of the families involved, I don't have a lot of patience on this one. If you've got something to say about the Linville murder, tell me now." Cramer was still bellowing.

"No, sir. You know that won't work."

"All right, then I'll come right over and you can tell me all about it."

"No again. If you come, you will be refused ad-mittance and the offer to attend tonight's gathering will be withdrawn."

There was exhaling on the other end that sounded as if it had the force to blow over a bookcase. "All right, nine o'clock?" I could tell Cramer was struggling to keep himself under control.

"Correct. Sergeant Stebbins or some other associate also will be welcome."

Cramer grumbled something that sounded like he'd bring Stebbins, and slammed down the phone.

"All right," I said to Wolfe. "Now, give me a fill-in." He did, and I have to admit I hadn't seen it, although I probably should have. He sketched out the evening and told me to reach Saul and Fred. "We could get by with only one of them," Wolfe said, "but both would be preferable."

My luck held. Saul had just come in from a job and Fred was at home and of course happy to get the call to action. Less than an hour later they were seated in the office, Fred with beer, which he drinks to please Wolfe, and Saul with Scotch, which he drinks to please himself. Wolfe gave them a quick fill-in on their roles, then excused himself and moved rapidly out of the office, a rare occurrence. At that, he was four minutes late for his afternoon appointment with the orchids.

TWENTY-TWO

Saul and Fred finished their drinks and left, and I went out to the kitchen to fill in Fritz in a general way about the plans for the evening. Fritz isn't big on knowing the details anyway; he's mainly just glad when a case ends. To him, that means we will be receiving the balance of whatever money Wolfe is owed and that he will again be eating normally. I never notice anything wrong with Wolfe's eating habits during a case, but Fritz insists that all the worrying he does over a solution has an extremely detrimental effect on his appetite and digestion.

In any event, when I left the kitchen Fritz was smiling. I then went back to the office and began setting it up for the evening, bringing in extra chairs and stocking the small serving table in the corner as a bar. I then tried to concentrate on getting some paperwork done at my desk, but as always happens when Wolfe is about to wrap up a case, I couldn't keep my mind focused. I finally gave up, told Fritz I was going out, and walked for more than an hour, turning the events of the day over in my mind and trying to anticipate what might go wrong tonight. Okay, so I'm a worrier by nature.

When I got home, Wolfe was back behind his desk, reading and drinking beer. I went up to my room, took a short nap, washed up, changed into a fresh shirt and tie, and came down just in time for dinner, which was beef braised in red wine and squash with sour cream. Wolfe's dinner-conversation was the new growth of racism in Europe, which he said could have been predicted twenty-five years ago by any clear-thinking sociologist. As usual, I mainly listened, most of my mind being on the activities that lay ahead.

After dinner, back in the office, I found myself looking at my watch every few minutes. Wolfe, on the other hand, was immersed in his book and seemed totally unconcerned about the time. At eight-fifty-two the doorbell rang and I went to answer it, seeing Doyle James through the one-way glass. "Come in," I said politely. "You're number one."

He saluted me with an index finger, smiled, and walked in. We went down the hall to the office, where he and Wolfe exchanged formal greetings. I directed him to a chair in the second row as the doorbell rang again. This was the big James contingent: Noreen, Michael, and Megan, along with Pamsett. None of them appeared to be particularly happy, although Michael was the glummest of the lot, which, given his current status, was understandable. Megan, dressed in basic black, was frowning, Pamsett looked puzzled, and Noreen gave me a tight, nervous smile. "This better be good—bloody damn good," Megan hissed under her breath as she went by me.

I ushered them into the office, steering Noreen to the red leather chair, placing Michael beside her and Megan next to her son, filling out the front row. I introduced Pamsett to Wolfe and directed him to a second-row spot beside Doyle James, who already had said hellos to his son and daughter and grunted at his ex-wife. He shook hands noncommittally with Pamsett.

The bell rang again, and this time Fritz got it, letting in Polly Mars, who was wearing a white blouse and a plaid wrap skirt that showed off her legs. She nodded grimly to me, still irked that she was missing a shooting session. I took her to the office, making introductions once again and pointing her at a second-row chair next to Pamsett, who nodded in her direction and fingered the knot of his blue-and-yellow-striped tie. By the time I went back to the hall, the bell had sounded yet again, this time rung by Rojek. When I opened the door, I found that Cramer and Stebbins were parked on the stoop too. As I was in the process of greeting them, Lily got out of a cab and, after tipping the driver, sashayed up the steps, acting as if everyone else had arrived unfashionably early.

I introduced her and the police to Rojek in the hall, and then steered everyone to the office, where I did still another round of name exchanges. Rojek, first looking at Noreen with a half-smile that got returned in kind, took one of the two remaining second-row seats, next to Polly, while Cramer and Stebbins, as they had so often in the past, settled into the two third-row chairs. Not surprisingly, the unexpected presence of the constabulary caused a hubbub among the others.

"Mr. Wolfe," Megan said, shaking a finger ornamented by a walnut-sized gem, "before another word is spoken in this room, I insist on an explanation as to why members of the police department are present. I understood this was a private investigation, initiated at the request of my daughter."

"And so it is, madam," Wolfe replied, shifting in his chair. "But it is the investigation of a capital crime, and I have invited the police to attend. Does this cause a problem for you?"

"It's . . . it's *irregular*," she said sharply, fixing Wolfe with a look meant to show that she was used to calling the shots in group settings.

"Perhaps, but Mr. Cramer and Mr. Stebbins are here as onlookers, not active participants. Unless, of course, their presence is required later."

That caused another stir, with everyone looking around nervously except Michael James, who kept his eyes fixed glumly at the orchid on Wolfe's desk. Megan didn't seem any happier than before, but this time she said nothing.

"Before we begin, will anyone have refreshments?" Wolfe asked. "As you can see, I am drinking beer."

Pamsett asked for a Scotch and water, and Rojek, surprisingly, piped up and ordered a bourbon on the rocks, both of which I mixed, but there were no other takers. Doyle James, looking even larger than usual in a black turtleneck sweater, grumbled that he hadn't realized he'd been invited to a cocktail party. Wolfe ignored him and made half the beer he had poured disappear, setting his glass firmly on the blotter. "As all of you are aware, my client is Miss James," he said, inclining his head in Noreen's direction. "Following Mr. Linville's death, she came to me with the entreaty that I find the means to exculpate her brother, and I of course told her that I could not guarantee such an eventuation." I suppressed a smirk; he was amusing himself with words again, this time by seeing how many ten-dollar ones beginning with the same letter he could cram into a single sentence.

"I did, however, agree to undertake an investigation, which I have now completed," Wolfe went on, his eyes moving from face to face.

"We're all certainly delighted to hear *that*," Cramer spat. "Do we get to hear the results in the next hour, or is this going to be one of your filibusters?"

"Sir, you are well aware that I prize economy of words. But I also place a high priority on precision and thoroughness—you of all people should appreciate that." Having thus disposed of the inspector, Wolfe turned his attention back to his beer, emptying the glass and refilling it from the second bottle.

"Almost from the beginning of Mr. Goodwin's and my inquiry, I was struck by a proliferation of coincidences. Let me enumerate these, not necessarily in chronological order: First, Mr. Linville's death occurred less than forty-eight hours after Mrs. James's return from an extended holiday in Europe. Second—"

"Just . . . a . . . minute!" Megan James rose half-way out of her chair like a 747 taking off. "If you're suggesting that I had anything to do with that man's death, you can—"

"I am suggesting nothing yet, madam," Wolfe said, glaring Megan back into her chair, "other than that we are faced with a series of coincidences. Now, if I may continue: Second, Doyle James, who says his visits to his Manhattan apartment are relatively rare, chose the night of Mr. Linville's death to remain in the city." Wolfe turned toward Doyle as if expecting another interruption, but got only a crooked smile from that ruddy face.

"Third, on that same night, Michael James was seen loitering on the sidewalk outside Mr. Linville's apartment building by the doorman."

"I wasn't loitering—I told both you and the police that," Michael said in an even voice, clenching a fist and bringing it down softly three times on the arm of his chair. "I was waiting for Linville. So I could . . . *talk* to him about . . . Noreen."

"All right, you were waiting," Wolfe said, turning a palm over. "I will not quibble over semantics. In any event—"

"Just a minute!" Cramer piped up. It was an evening for interruptions. "That last should hardly be called a coincidence. It's just one more piece of evidence that James had been stalking Linville."

Wolfe, obviously irked, drew in air and released it slowly. "Inspector, I ask your indulgence, please. I am proceeding as if this gentleman were innocent. If you will allow that assumption to stand for the moment, his being in front of the building on that particular night *was* coincidental to the death of Mr. Linville. You, sir, passionately wish for a brief session, yet you persist in prolonging the evening. Continuing on to yet a fourth coincidence: With the possible exception of Miss Rowan, not one of you in this room—Misses James and Mars, Mrs. James, Messrs. Rojek, Pamsett, James, and James—is able to account for all of your time last Wednesday night. In particular, none of you has a witness to your whereabouts between midnight and one o'clock, the period during which, it is estimated by the medical examiner, Mr. Linville was murdered."

"What's so unusual about that?" Rojeck cut in, clearing his throat. "Most nights I'm home between midnight and one, but I can't prove it because I live alone."

Wolfe ignored him. "I weighed these occurrences and concluded that, taken both individually and collectively, they were plausible. But there was still another coincidence, one that I could not so easily dismiss. And although I was aware of it before any of those I just enumerated, it was the last to intrude upon my consciousness."

Wolfe sighed and lifted his shoulders a full half-inch, dropping them and allowing himself another deep breath. "Sir," he said to Inspector Cramer, "I wish now to publicly apologize for a comment I made to you in this room several days ago. When you mentioned Mr. Goodwin's confrontation with Mr. Linville on the sidewalk in front of the establishment known as Morgana's, I cavalierly shrugged it off, stating there was no connection between that meeting and Mr. Linville's death a few hours later. Regrettably, I was in error."

If he didn't have it before, Wolfe now held the total attention of the gathering, with most of them—including Lily—casting glances in my direction. I kept my face down, focusing on my notebook, lest I destroy the mood of the moment.

"I'm interested in that error," Cramer said in a hoarse voice.

"With good reason," Wolfe responded glumly. "My chagrin is of course palpable, my embarrassment manifest."

"Of course," Purley Stebbins piped up, and damned if Cramer didn't glare at him and tell him to button his lip.

"Some of you by now likely have perceived the importance of that sidewalk meeting," Wolfe went on.

"And some of us may be just a tad denser than you seem to be giving us credit for," Doyle James put in with a scowl. "I for one am not ashamed to admit that I haven't got the foggiest idea where you're heading with this damned business about Morgana's."

"I have to agree," Pamsett seconded almost cheerfully, playing once again with the knot of his tie. "Are we to believe that—"

"Oh, get with it, both of you!" It was Megan, ready again to lift off the tarmac. "Can't you see that he's posturing? He's got an audience and he loves it, but it's obvious that he's just blowing smoke around. I think we're all wasting our time here." Speaking of smoke, Megan obviously was dying for a cigarette, which wasn't helping her disposition any.

Noreen, who had been staring at her lap almost since she sat down, looked at her mother angrily and started to say something, but Wolfe cut her off.

"Madam, the last thing I want to do is waste time—mine or that of any of you," he said as he reached under his desk for the buzzer. "It is far too precious a commodity to be squandered, and as Shakespeare's second King Richard said, 'I wasted time, and now doth time waste me'—ah, Saul, Fred, please come in, and bring our guest."

Every face turned toward the doorway. Saul Panzer and Fred Durkin stood on either side of Todd Halliburton, who wore a bewildered look as he looked over the crowd. "Hey, I thought I was here to see just Nero Wolfe," he snarled, wheeling on Saul.

"Mr. Halliburton, if you please," Wolfe said, holding up a palm. "I am Nero Wolfe. You are indeed here to see me. I thank you for coming. I will explain the presence of these people momentarily; I don't believe you have met them, other than Misses James and Mars, Inspector Cramer, and of course Mr. Goodwin here, whom I'm sure you recognize." With that, he introduced our other guests, including Stebbins, nodding toward each in turn, and then motioning Halliburton to the remaining empty chair in the second row while both Saul and Fred remained standing. The little jerk sat, but looked uncomfortable, which bothered me not even a little.

"Sir," Wolfe said, shifting to face him, "the purpose of this gathering is to discuss the violent death of your friend Mr. Linville. I regret having Mr. Panzer and Mr. Durkin escort you here through artifice, but I deemed your presence essential and your assistance an invaluable part of our discussion."

"Artifice? They damn near dragged me!" Halliburton howled.

"This the kid who was Linville's great buddy?" It was Doyle James, who turned in his seat and shot a glare Halliburton's way.

"That is correct," Wolfe replied. "And he also is the individual who recognized Mr. Goodwin after the now-infamous sidewalk encounter."

"So what?" Megan snapped.

"As I am trying to demonstrate, that meeting was significant," Wolfe said, pouring the remaining beer from his second bottle and watching the foam dissipate. "The reason Inspector Cramer knew Mr. Goodwin had confronted Barton Linville is that he learned it from Mr. Halliburton here."

"That's not so surprising, is it?" asked Douglas Rojek. "I mean, Goodwin's picture has been in the paper quite a few times. I remember seeing it—and yours, too, of course."

"It is no doubt true that Mr. Goodwin has become recognizable to at least a substantial minority of New York's newspaper-reading populace, including Mr. Halliburton," Wolfe conceded. "I would like now to turn to Miss James. When she first visited this office, I asked her, among other questions, whether Mr. Linville knew her aunt, Miss Rowan, and I received an affirmative reply. Is that not correct?"

"Yes," Noreen said, nodding nervously and swallowing. "They met once, maybe twice."

"Twice," Lily cut in coldly.

"Just so. And then I asked if Mr. Linville had

been aware that Miss Rowan and Mr. Goodwin were close friends. Your reply?" Wolfe dipped his head in Noreen's direction.

"I said I thought it came up in conversation, but I honestly can't remember any details."

Wolfe touched a finger to the side of his nose. "Mr. Halliburton, had you been aware of the friendship between Miss Rowan and Mr. Goodwin before the subject arose a moment ago?"

"No . . . why should I? And why should I care?" he answered with a sneer, crossing his arms over his chest.

"No reason," Wolfe said blandly, placing both hands on his desk blotter, palms down, then shifting his attention to Noreen. "Miss James, you hired me to prove your brother's innocence in the death of Barton Linville. As I warned you when I accepted that commission, I could not guarantee success. Indeed, when I am through tonight, you may well feel I have not succeeded. If that is the case, it goes without saying that you will receive no bill. And now—"

"Hold it right there," Cramer said, putting equal stress on each word. "Do you mean to say you dragged all of us here for nothing?"

"That is not what I said, sir. But it is true that you may well term my reconstruction of events conjecture. Let us now return to the last evening of Mr. Linville's life," Wolfe said, starting in on a fresh beer that Fritz had delivered during the noisy intermission. "Mr. Linville and his friend Mr. Halliburton here had gone to Morgana's and departed about ten-twenty. Is that correct, sir?"

"Yes," Halliburton muttered sulkily. "I've told the police that."

"So you have. An angry Mr. Goodwin, seeking a confrontation with Mr. Linville over his alleged attack of Miss James, was waiting for them outside, and words were exchanged, with both Mr. Linville and Mr. Halliburton overtly resentful of Mr. Goodwin's

presence. The doorman interceded, and Mr. Goodwin—"

"Who tried to slug me!"

"—and Mr. Goodwin withdrew," Wolfe finished
his sentence, glaring at Halliburton. I got the feeling
that Wolfe would like to slug the next person who
interrupted him.

"Messrs. Linville and Halliburton left together,
and, as Mr. Halliburton told Mr. Goodwin, they went
on foot to another establishment several blocks away,
where they had a few drinks before parting at . . .
what time was it, Mr. Halliburton?"

"I told Goodwin, something like eleven-thirty or
thereabouts. I told the police too," Halliburton whin-
nied, looking over his shoulder in Cramer's direction.
"It seems like we're doing a hell of a lot of repeating
here."

"So you were together for at least seventy minutes
after the confrontation with Mr. Goodwin," Wolfe
said, ignoring the complaint. "And you had recognized Mr. Goodwin immediately?"

"Yeah. I've said that before too."

"But Mr. Linville had not recognized him?"

"Seems like you're telling it."

"I'd like to hear it again from you, sir."

Halliburton took a breath and clenched his teeth.
"Sparky didn't recognize Goodwin. He'd never met
him and I guess he'd never seen his picture—or if he
had, it didn't register. Satisfied?"

"Thank you," Wolfe said, his eyes sweeping the
room. "Let me now suggest what transpired after Mr.
Linville and Mr. Halliburton walked away from Morgana's. Mr. Halliburton was probably quick to point
out that their harasser had been none other than
Archie Goodwin, the well-known private investigator.
At which point Mr. Linville, who was known to indulge in braggadocio over what he considered his
amorous exploits, made the connection, boasting to
his companion that Mr. Goodwin must have been

seeking some form of reprisal because of the forcible advances he, Linville, had made to the niece of Mr. Goodwin's longtime friend Miss Rowan."

"You're just guessing," Halliburton snorted.

"An educated guess. What Mr. Linville said, and the insolent way in which he said it, enraged you, sir."

"Why the hell should it enrage me?" Halliburton shot back, sitting up straight and squaring his shoulders. "What Sparky did was his business. He had his life and I had mine."

"You also had something in common, however, and that was that you both knew Miss James. But while Mr. Linville's relationship with her had been characterized by violence and, ultimately on her part, loathing, yours was one of affection, albeit unrequited."

"I don't know where you got that," Halliburton squeaked, looking at the tips of his shoes. His ears were redder than Cramer's face had been earlier.

"I got it from Mr. Goodwin's observations of your reactions when he visited you yesterday," Wolfe said. "He reported that your feelings for the young woman were perspicuous."

"Hallie didn't say anything to *me* about his feelings," Noreen put in. "In fact, we only met a couple of times."

"You hear that, Wolfe?" Cramer snapped. "How could this guy"—he gestured toward Halliburton—"have been so worked up if they barely knew each other?"

Wolfe considered him dourly. "Did not the young Dante see his Beatrice but twice? Yet that was enough to stir a passion that belongs to the ages. Likely, Mr. Halliburton did not express his feelings because he doubted their reciprocation. In any event, he held Miss James in high esteem, and when he learned from his friend of a conquest that—"

"God, do we have to go into this much detail?" It was Lily, grimacing.

Wolfe considered her, leaned back, and closed

his eyes for ten seconds. "Madam," he asked Noreen, "do you wish me to continue, or do you feel I have shown disdain for propriety?"

"No—please go on. It's all right, Aunt Lily," she said, struggling to control her facial expression. "I've been getting myself ready for something like this for a long time. I'm okay . . . really." Lily sent her the kind of smile I've gotten from the same source several times when I was particularly dejected. I hoped it worked as well for Noreen as it has for me.

Wolfe leaned forward, looking from face to face, eyes wide. "I have a client," he said acidly, "and I intend to represent her. Does anyone dispute or challenge that intention?"

The room was quiet—including Cramer, who looked as if he wanted to chew up a whole box of cigars. "Very well," Wolfe went on, "as I started to say, when Mr. Halliburton learned of his friend's escapade, he became enraged, at least internally. I daresay within seconds after he heard the story, he began planning violent action. And—"

"This stinks!" Halliburton shouted, tacking on the same word he had used that night in front of Morgana's. But while I had started to take a swing at him for such talk, Wolfe reacted by bending down behind his desk—no easy feat for someone of his configuration. When he reappeared, he was holding the tire iron I had gotten from the trunk of the Mercedes. He had wrapped it in one of his handkerchiefs so that his hand did not come in contact with the metal, and he set it carefully on his blotter without a word, turning back to Halliburton.

"Now, sir," he said, "as I was about to—"

"What's . . . that?" The kid's eyes were so wide I could see white all around the irises.

"A tire iron, of course. Now, as—"

"No-o-o!" Halliburton sprang to his feet, wailing. "You can't prove it! You don't know what really happened. You had to be there. Sparky kept on bragging that he did ... You know, he was a ... When I hit him with that thing, he ..." He was babbling, then hyperventilating, his eyes darting from face to face, his palms up. "Noreen, I ... I ..." He ran down like a music box in need of winding and stood in front of her, tears streaming down his cheeks. Purley Stebbins, who had leapt to Halliburton's side the instant he popped up, was now calmly giving him the "You-have-the-right-to-remain-silent ..." spiel while getting his cuffs ready.

Noreen went around Halliburton to her brother and knelt in front of him, burying her face in his lap and sobbing, while Doyle James stood over her silently, an arm on her shoulder. Megan was crying now too, and so was Lily. Waterworks from any one of them would have unsettled Wolfe, but all this was more than enough to drive him from the room. He was barely noticed as he rose, moved around his desk, and marched into the hall, turning toward the kitchen. That's just like him, leaving me to mop up his messes.

TWENTY-THREE

"That was a pretty sleazy stunt with the tire iron," Cramer said, leaning back in the red leather chair and taking a healthy swallow of beer. "I should have known you were up to something when you asked to have Goodwin get a look at the piece of metal that was used on Linville."

The creases in Wolfe's cheeks deepened, which for him is a smile. He was feeling good now, some fifteen hours after putting the finger on Todd Halliburton. When the tension had abated last night and most of our guests had left, Wolfe returned to his office and was handed a check by Doyle James on behalf of his daughter, which I deposited this morning at our neighborhood branch of the Metropolitan Trust Company. And now, at twelve-forty, after his morning frolic upstairs with his orchids, he was anticipating the baked scallops that he'd be consuming in less than an hour.

"Come, Inspector," he said, "surely you have on occasion employed even sleazier stunts, to use your terminology."

"Whatever works—within the law, of course," Cramer said defensively.

"Precisely. And as you no doubt are aware, I would not have used the artifice I did had the guilty individual been, say, Mrs. James, or Mr. Pamsett, or even Doyle James. They would not have reacted satisfactorily for my—or perhaps I should say our—purposes. But it was clear to me, having had Mr. Halliburton described in such detail to me by Mr. Goodwin, that his emotional constitution made him particularly vulnerable to this approach."

"Well, it sure as hell worked," Cramer conceded without even a trace of resentment in his voice. "You've got to feel pretty good about this one. And for that matter, so do I, for reasons we both know. And to top everything off, after we took Halliburton downtown, he babbled damn near all night about how he'd wasted Linville—who supposedly had been his friend, for God's sake. In fact, the more he talked, the prouder he sounded; I think he's convinced that he did society a service. He refused counsel, and the poor guy brought in from the public defender's office to represent him couldn't shut him up. The kid wants his trial tomorrow so he can plead guilty to any charge and get it over with. Doesn't seem to care what happens to him."

"The murderer as self-styled hero," Wolfe observed. "Not an altogether unusual reaction. Mr. Cramer, I invite you to join us for lunch. We're having baked scallops."

Cramer squinted at his beer glass before drinking. "You know, that's the best offer I've had in weeks," he said, turning to me and winking.

"Archie, please tell Fritz to put on another plate," Wolfe said. Which goes to show just how good a mood he really was in.

TWENTY-FOUR

As I had promised, the *Gazette* got its scoop. I called Lon Monday night after the dust cleared, finally reaching him at home, and gave him the details plus plenty of color and several quotes from Wolfe. It made for good reading in the Tuesday afternoon edition, which Wolfe and I both devoured after Cramer left, his belly full of scallops. Seeing as how the story broke too late for the morning papers, the *Gazette* gave it especially big play, with an upper-case banner headline reading NEW CONFESSION IN LINVILLE CASE! along with a major story, two sidebars, and lots of pictures, including one of Wolfe with a caption that referred to him as a "master sleuth."

Halliburton's family eventually found him a big-time defense lawyer who managed to make an insanity plea hold up, which didn't go down well with the press or Linville's family, to say nothing of the D.A.'s office. He is now boarding with the state at one of its high-security facilities for the mentally disturbed.

After the hubbub surrounding the trial died down, Michael James admitted to his family that he had indeed fabricated his story because of his fear that one of them—he wouldn't say which he thought it was—had killed Linville to avenge Noreen. One piece of positive fallout, according to Lily, is that Michael and his mother were tearfully reconciled and seem to be getting along better than they have in years.

Noreen appears to have recovered from her own

trauma nicely, which is all the more surprising considering that her ordeal got spread all over the press and TV. She dropped Rojek soon after Halliburton's trial, telling her aunt that she thought he was "too shallow." And now, Lily tells me, she's about to take a new job with a publishing company in Chicago, which has offered her far greater editing responsibilities than she ever had with Melbourne Books. "I'll miss Noreen, but it'll do her good to get away from New York—and particularly her mother," was Lily's observation.

I certainly can't disagree with that.